"Why are *you* here?"

"I had a dream about you. I was worried. Hell, Nicole, you're my wife." David glanced over the damage done by the quake. One side of Nicole's building had given way; four floors had fallen like a house of cards into the basement. Fortunately, he'd not only rescued Nicole, but the baby in her arms, too. "Were you baby-sitting or something?" he finally asked.

"No, I..." What could Nicole say to the father of her child, to explain the fact that she'd never told him about Matthew? "I'm not baby-sitting," she said at last.

"You're not?" Suddenly David stared in amazement at the child in his estranged wife's arms. "Guess the real problem is that I didn't get here a lot sooner," he said.

"This is Matthew, your son," Nicole returned.

Dear Reader,

Déjà Vu, which was published in July, 1990, was one of the most enjoyable books I've written for Harlequin Intrigue, and I was overjoyed to have the opportunity to revisit the characters in *The Dreamer's Kiss*. It's been a true pleasure to "return to the scene of the crime" and be a part of Intrigue's Tenth Anniversary Celebration.

Needless to say, much has happened to my two favorite characters—Nicole and David—since their appearance in *Déjà Vu*. They were married at the end of that book, and now have lived through both the birth of a baby and a separation. Now, in *The Dreamer's Kiss*, they have the opportunity to get back together again!

I hope you enjoy reading their story as much as I've enjoyed writing it!

Sincerely,

Laura Pender

Laura Pender

Laura Pender
The Dreamer's Kiss

Harlequin Books

TORONTO • NEW YORK • LONDON
AMSTERDAM • PARIS • SYDNEY • HAMBURG
STOCKHOLM • ATHENS • TOKYO • MILAN
MADRID • WARSAW • BUDAPEST • AUCKLAND

ISBN 0-373-22292-0

THE DREAMER'S KISS

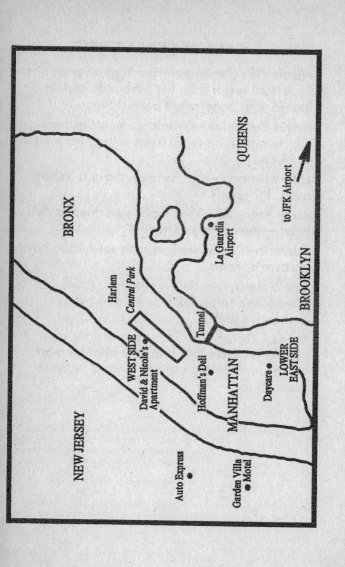

CAST OF CHARACTERS

Nicole Ellis Germaine—She kept a very important secret from her husband...but now feared their baby might be in danger.

David Germaine—Within moments of seeing Nicole again, he realized he should have kept in touch.

Little Matthew—Did he really have a father now...for good?

Jerry Brunsold—Was David's partner really helping the estranged family?

Dominic—The mysterious man seemed to have his own agenda.

Garth Donnely—He'd destroyed David Germaine's ship...but was he also out to destroy his life?

Morley Kroft—The Germaines are the only people who can help him find what he most wants...and he'd go to any lengths to make them do so.

Prologue

Hoffman's Delicatessen began business in lower Manhattan under the ownership of Emil Hoffman in 1922. Under son Carl's management since 1955, the Hoffman family's landmark establishment has remained at its original location, continuing to offer the same renowned food specialties. The family always lived in a roomy apartment over the deli. Even when Manhattan real estate went through the roof, the Hoffman family remained downtown.

But Marion Hoffman was thinking of finding a different place to live lately. The sixty-eight-year-old woman, who ran the deli so efficiently with her husband, Carl, and their granddaughter and her husband, was tired and thinking more and more seriously about Florida or Phoenix these days. But it wasn't the work or the customers, the hustle of the lunch trade or the myriad jobs behind the scenes that had brought her to this idea. It was the dreams. After nearly forty years in the business, nightmares were telling her to get out.

She couldn't tell Carl about the dreams; he'd only laugh and tell her that maybe she should begin taking her lunches from their new selection of yogurts and other health foods, rather than the pastrami. Marion knew her diet wasn't the problem. So she kept her dreams to herself and tried to figure out the meaning behind them, and why they seemed so real. In fact, her dreams seemed more like memories. . . .

IT WAS ALWAYS THE SAME. She was standing in her place behind the counter and looking through the front window at the rain falling on the Manhattan streets. Their lunch trade was off, due to the rain and deliveries were up for the same reason.

It was raining, and everything seemed so real. Mr. Grizwald, owner of the tuxedo shop across the street, was there standing behind his own shop window, staring at the rain as though willing it to change.

She had just sent the delivery kid out with three orders, and was standing behind the counter watching two people running toward the door, both hunched over in the rain. The woman, wearing a tan raincoat, was crossing the street, while a man in a dark topcoat was running along the front of the store. They met at the door and paused, talking.

Marion smiled; at least there would be a small bit of life in the deli this lunch hour. But a third man was approaching them before the window. He was running toward them, wearing a raincoat, hat and sunglasses, a hate-filled expression on what little was visible of his face. Suddenly it seemed that her vision was filled with the man, and she was watching frozen as he came up to the people standing at the door in the rain.

She saw the gun in his hand, and the sound of it firing reverberated in her head as the woman stumbled and fell, her coat falling open as she slumped to the pavement, a bright red stain of blood spoiling the paisley print dress she was wearing.

Mr. Grizwald was shouting then, and Marion was reaching for the telephone to call for help. But the man and woman were gone. It was as though they had never been there at all.

Still, she and Mr. Grizwald had seen them. They stared at each other without speaking for a long time before she turned and looked at the calendar on the wall behind the counter. It was September 6.

And then the dream faded away, only to begin again, exactly the same as before.

What was important about September 6? She didn't know, but the dream that recurred every night seemed to be telling her that something bad would happen then. September was still three months away, but Marion Hoffman was beginning to feel that she'd rather be out of the city when the date finally arrived.

ACROSS THE CONTINENT from Marion, in Carmel-by-the-Sea, California, Nicole Ellis Germaine could have told Marion Hoffman not to worry about the coming September 6. The date she was dreaming of was nearly three years past already. But perhaps Nicole's explanation of the dreams would have been more troubling than her current fear that they were a premonition. For they weren't dreams at all; they were memories.

For Nicole, the memories remained constantly in mind. She was the woman who had been shot in front of Hoffman's Deli on September 6 three years before. And the man she had been speaking to was the man who became her husband, David Germaine. What happened after the shooting would be beyond belief if she hadn't lived through it, however, and Nicole still had moments when she doubted that any of it had happened.

The bullet had been intended for David Germaine, a world famous oceanographer, but Nicole had seen the gun first and jumped in the way. She had saved his life, and the two of them had been given a strange opportunity to save hers.

She and David had been taken back in time one week before the impact of that bullet. They had been given a chance to uncover the plot against him and avoid the fatal shot. In so doing, they had found love together.

Now, if it weren't for her son, Matthew, she might be convinced that it was a dream. But it wasn't a dream, and her son was the constant reminder of the marriage that she had left behind her before his birth.

Nicole could empathize with the problems Marion was having with her sleep, however. She, too, had been plagued by dreams over the past weeks. And she, too, was beginning to worry that something terrible was about to happen.

Her dreams seemed to be telling her so.

Chapter One

Everything was shaking: the floor, the shelves of books and knickknacks and the plants filling the space below the front window were all vibrating as though an electric current were running through the room to jolt them all into motion. Her bed, too, was vibrating, building to a tumultuous rocking, until the legs began thumping against the hardwood floor.

Nicole Ellis clung to the brass headboard, her body bouncing up from the disheveled bedding, her legs kicking frantically against the force that drove her bed into its frenetic dance.

She heard a siren wailing nearby as the books began to topple from their shelves, her records and CDs flying out to skitter across the floor. The wail grew louder, piercingly close, until she realized that it wasn't a siren but her own cry of fear and pain that she was hearing.

Suddenly, the bed stopped moving. All was still. Then she could hear Matthew crying in the next room. It hadn't been her at all, but the baby wanting to be fed. Nicole rose from her bed and stumbled sleepily out of her room, thanking God that it had all been a dream.

She entered her fourteen-month-old son's room and gathered him up to her, silencing his cries with her presence. Then she filled a bottle for him and took him back to her room to lie against her breast, their communion bringing calm to both of them once more.

NICOLE WOKE LATER, lying in her bed with Matthew cradled in her arms. She shifted slightly, causing him to stir in his sleep. He lifted his small fingers and fumbled at his mouth for a moment, squeezing his eyes tighter. Nicole kissed the sleeping child's forehead lightly, smiling, and then she snuggled down into her pillow and closed her eyes once more.

A BEARDED MAN stood before her, indistinct within a fog that swirled around and over him. His dark-blond hair was long, and it streamed to the side in the wind, even as he seemed to be moving toward her. His icy blue eyes bored into her from within the weather-worn mask of his face.

And then he spoke, in a voice like a cold wind howling over the sea, saying, "Not safe anywhere!" And his eyes seemed to swell, growing to engulf the face and become a whole world of raging storm and swelling seas. A roaring gale of wind and bursting sea flowed over her, washing her away into the depths of icy water and onto a rocky beach.

She stood amid the rocks, staring out at the retreating sea until the mist rolled in to shroud it in gray.

And then there was nothing.

And Matthew was waking in her arms, kicking his little feet against her hip as they lay together in the brightening dawn.

NICOLE ELLIS GERMAINE left the brightly colored confines of the university day-care center with a frown tugging at the corners of her full lips and darkening the expression in her intelligent hazel eyes. She felt a new sense of dread at the thought of leaving her infant in the care of strangers for even the few hours she spent in class every day. It was a feeling that had grown over time, each day becoming a bit more of a weight on her heart. She felt as though she were doing something wrong in some way, and that the child was in danger there. It was fear that she felt for him, plain and simple.

But, of course, there was no reason for such feelings. The University of California campus at Carmel-by-the-Sea was small and secure, and the day-care facilities were top-rate. Nothing would happen to him there, and no one could get in to harm him.

Still, she felt afraid for him.

And, though it was a foolish feeling to have when she was only a month away from graduation, Nicole felt guilty about her class work, as well as afraid for her child. Strangely enough, however, Nicole's guilt didn't seem to be about the baby. She knew that Matthew would have a far better life if his mother had a degree and a career; that was indisputable. No, the guilt was a general sort of feeling that didn't seem to have any real focus. She felt as though she had left something undone.

Nicole concluded that her dreams were influencing her mood. The recurring dream of the earthquake and the man by the sea couldn't help but have an effect on her waking life, could it? It wasn't a regular dream, but once or twice a week it would replay in her sleeping mind, waking her to lie in fear until she could convince herself that it was, indeed, only a dream. She'd had the dream the past two nights, and she dreaded going to sleep tonight.

It was strange to feel such foreboding on so beautiful a spring day. The breeze coming in from the ocean, a mile away, was warm and carried the scent of salt air to the beautifully green college campus, and students were walking to and from their classes with light steps and smiles on their faces. It seemed obvious that nothing could possibly be wrong on a day like this.

Still, she felt trepidation as she walked to her morning class, and the feeling was distracting her from the studies that should be her prime focus. Little more than a month from now, she would have her law degree. After twelve years of intermittent study, Nicole's schooling would be done. That was worrisome, too, for it meant leaving the security of academia for the insecurities of the wide world.

Then she would have to face the bar exam.

Not that she really had to face any of that, of course. Lingering at the back of her mind was the thought that she could always go back to David. He would surely welcome her back.

But she didn't necessarily want to go back, and she surely wouldn't go without her degree. Not after she'd come this far. Still, she felt an emptiness within her that seemed ready-made for his form, and the closer she got to achieving her dreams, the more she missed him.

Maybe, if she hadn't been so adamant about him staying away, he'd be here now. They might have found a way to patch things up. Maybe, if she'd just relented...

"Hey, Nicole!" A young woman shouted out behind her, breaking her gloomy train of thought, and she turned to greet the small blonde who trotted up to her.

"Did you finish that paper?" Gail Kavanaugh, a fellow senior, stopped at her side, a rather pensive look on her face. "What precedent did you use for Kellerman v. California?" She hovered beside her, seeming to wait for a response before breathing.

"I didn't use any," she said. "The whole thing was prior restraint of trade." She couldn't help but smile at the young woman's rather worried enthusiasm.

"But you didn't list any precedent? Conway v. New York?" She spoke eagerly, waiting for confirmation from Nicole, as though she were the instructor, rather than just another student.

"I suppose you could," Nicole said as they resumed walking toward their class building. "But I don't see the point. Prior restraint is illegal in itself, so there's no need of a great volume of precedents to support the case, Gail. Why are you so worried about that?"

"Oh, I've got eight precedents supporting the defense arguments," the young woman said. "I probably overdid it. Nearly fifty pages."

"Fifty?"

"Is that too long, do you think? Is she going to knock me down for being wordy?"

"I wouldn't know about that, Gail. You do seem to overreact to assignments, though."

"I want to make sure I'm covered from every angle," she explained. "And I'm afraid I end up looking like an anal-retentive twerp."

"You don't, either."

"Come on, Nicole, fifty pages? She'll fall asleep halfway through. How long is your paper?"

"Sixteen pages."

"Sixteen? See, I'm dead. She always likes your papers, and they're always short."

"My papers are short because I've got a baby to take care of," Nicole explained. "That's hardly a scholarly reason."

"It doesn't matter why," the glum young woman said, throwing open the door of the red brick law building. "It only matters that she likes your papers the way they are."

"Wait a second," Nicole said, stopping her companion from entering the building. "Glance back at that guy by the bench. Have you seen him before?"

Gail turned slightly and looked quickly, as Nicole had asked, then turned back at her. "No," she said. "I've never seen him before. Why?"

"Probably nothing," Nicole admitted as she walked into the building. "I've just seen him around several times over the past couple days. Don't worry about it. You know," she said, continuing with their previous conversation, "Professor Arndt has got to be impressed with anyone who could find eight precedents for the case.''

"Maybe I need a baby to help me trim my reports," Gail said seriously, as she looked at her closely. Gail laughed then, shaking her head. "Well, I can't help it now. How is your little knucklehead?"

"He's fine. Getting into more things every day. How is your shin?" Matthew had gleefully pushed a stack of law books over against Gail's leg at a study session a couple nights earlier.

"I've stopped limping," she said. "It's my own fault for not running when I saw him headed my way."

"I'm sure it's just a phase he's going through," Nicole said. "He's into everything, and it's wearing me out."

"He's just curious."

"I don't remember being that curious. At least my parents never mentioned it," Nicole said, pausing outside the door to their classroom.

"They didn't want to scare you. Besides, he probably takes after his..." But Gail let it trail off, because she'd never been sure exactly what Nicole's relationship was with her husband, and didn't want to put her foot into anything. "Well," she said then, "here we are at the scene of my execution."

Gail threw the door open and held it for Nicole, entering after her, to find to her dismay that Professor Arndt was at her desk already. Nicole dropped her paper on top of the stack, with a pleasant "Good morning" to the gray-haired woman at the desk, and took a seat.

"Oh, good." Professor Arndt looked over her half glasses at Gail as she put her paper down. "I was looking forward to reading a nice long book this evening," she said. "I knew I could rely on your research to provide one, Ms. Kavanaugh."

"Well, I—"

The woman cut her off, smiling. "No you needn't explain. I appreciate a lawyer who does her homework. But you must realize that you don't have to present every word of it in court. A bored judge is more likely to rule against you. Right?"

"Right," Gail agreed, escaping to a place beside Nicole. "I'm dead," she told her. "Five years down the drain."

NICOLE'S DAY WENT WELL. Her classes seemed to be getting easier as she neared graduation. At times she couldn't believe she was here at all. She'd begun her studies over twelve years ago, an eighteen-year-old freshman at NYU studying prelaw and planning a crusading career as a consumer advocate or some other vaguely helpful position. She hadn't been sure of anything then, only that she thought the law should help people.

Then her father had died, and she had had to work to help her family out and obtain the money to continue her studies. She had continued in that manner, working as a legal secretary for Clint Forrester at his firm in New York City.

She had been doing well, until the fateful day in September nearly three years ago when her life had been blown apart and time had literally stood still for her. David Germaine had been at the center of everything. They had worked together solving the mystery confronting them, and their union had seemed to be fated from the start.

David Germaine had been there, and he could be here now. All she had to do was pick up the phone.

Walking home from the day-care with young Matthew in his pack on her back—cooing animal sounds into her ear as he gently tugged at her dark brown hair—she felt as though she might cry.

A moment's pain and a rash argument had driven her from her husband, nothing more than that. She had been foolish to leave, and had told herself that over and over again. Call him, her inner voice had said, but she'd stubbornly refused to listen to that voice. And the longer she put the call off, the harder it was to make it.

But why should she call him, anyway? He hadn't wanted a child, and yet here his child was, cooing gently in her ear. Matthew was the baby that he hadn't wanted, and she would be damned if she would crawl back to him to live off his good graces. Not without her own career, her own income. If she went back, it would be on her own terms.

DAVID GERMAINE stood at the wheel of the *Katharine,* his oceanographic yacht, and watched the whitecapped waves rushing against the bow of the ship. The wind blew his sandy hair back, like a pennant made ragged by the ravages of the weather, and salt spray stung at his blue eyes and frosted his beard as he stared into the storm.

They had rounded Cape Horn several days before, but they were still beset by storms as they passed along the California coast. Even now, though they were nearly to their destination, the wind was bitterly cold and waves crested over twelve feet. His ship rolled with the swells, sending his crew of two young oceanographers down to their cabins to ride out their seasickness, while his partner, Jerry Brunsvold, sat with the charts in the wheelhouse. They were traveling under the power of their engines, rather than using the sails in the storm, yet he had chosen to stand here amid the elements and face their fury, rather than pilot them from the warmth of the forward wheelhouse, where Jerry sat, perfectly dry. He had stubbornly decided to sail around the Cape instead of going through the Panama Canal, as any sensible ship's captain would have done, just as he stubbornly faced tonight's storm.

David didn't feel sensible. He felt rash and foolish, and more than a little bit angry. And, though he wasn't yet sure of the cause, he was scared.

No, he was sure of the cause, he admitted to himself. It was the dreams that scared him. Horrible dreams in which buildings were toppled, and the cries of those caught within rose up to color the air with pain. He heard a baby crying in the dream, though he didn't know why. And he had seen Nicole lying dead in the rubble.

Nicole.

That was all he needed to drive him to her. No matter the doubtful logic of following a dream; no matter the question of whether she wanted him there or not; he had seen her dead, and that was all that mattered.

He could not ignore such a warning, no matter how otherworldly the source.

Besides, they had met in a vortex of time, hadn't they? Nicole had been shot protecting him from a murderer's bullet, and time had leapt back for them, to provide them with a second chance. A whole week of their lives had replayed itself, just so that Nicole might live and they might be together. After an experience like that, nothing was unbelievable.

Almost nothing. It was unbelievable to him that they weren't together now. It was unbelievable to him that she had left him without a satisfactory explanation and demanded that he stay away. That was unbelievable.

He had honored all of her demands on him, save one. He had not gone along with a divorce when she brought it up, and wouldn't until she could prove that it was really necessary. Fortunately, she hadn't pushed the issue.

He found hope in that fact.

They had nearly reached the Cape before he had the first dream, and though he cursed himself now, their course was set, and they had to follow it. So they had traveled through the icy, storm-tossed waters and begun their journey north toward summer with David feeling more and more certain they would be too late.

He had seen Nicole dead in his dreams!

The more he thought of those dreams, the more he suffered pangs of guilt. Since she had left him, there had been times when he allowed himself to ponder what it would have been like if she had simply died from the gunshot that fateful September day. He wouldn't have known he loved her, and they wouldn't have gotten married—and he wouldn't be so bitterly lonely today.

But he would probably still be in mourning for his first wife, killed by a drunken driver when he was at sea, and wouldn't have known that love was possible for him again. He wouldn't have known their blissful year at sea, either. He wouldn't have known the taste of her kisses or felt her miraculous body next to his or had the opportunity to listen to the music of her voice. He would have remained a stoic widower living on his boat, living for his work.

But that was exactly what he was now, wasn't it?

What had he done to drive her away? He still wasn't sure. He wished he could remember his exact words, so that he could find the pain in them. He wished he could have put a knife in his own heart, rather than utter such words. But he couldn't remember them.

He remembered the argument. He remembered the days when she had been increasingly silent toward him. And he remembered the day she had left the ship for good. He had said some horrid things to her; he could remember that well enough. But all husbands and wives had words from time to time. What puzzled him was the sudden and fierce enmity she had showed him, which she refused to explain.

Now he watched the roaring waves, the wind blasting into his bearded face. She probably wouldn't recognize him as he was now. He had allowed his hair to grow past his shoulder, and had stopped shaving months ago. His appearance didn't really matter, anyway, for there was no one to please or impress out here. He imagined that he looked rather like the captain of a renegade vessel scavenging the sea two hundred years ago, rather than a respected twentieth-century scientist.

He piloted the ship through the night, across the stormy sea, toward his wife, who had exiled herself to California. He was racing the waves and the wind and time itself to arrive before his dreams could come true.

They were less than an hour away now, but he feared he might still be too late.

Nicole was dead in his dreams!

NICOLE SLEPT FITFULLY that night. Matthew had been fussy, with a tooth coming in, and he had kept her up later than she would have liked. But she hadn't been eager to sleep anyway. She was certain that she would have the dream again, and she didn't want to face the uncertain omens of her dreams.

The arrival of another tooth had prompted greater sadness, too. She couldn't help but feel that Matthew's father should be there. David was missing his son's progress because of her.

But then, he hadn't wanted children, had he? This guilt she felt was a reflex based on her own feelings, not his.

She should have gotten to know more about him before marrying him. Love alone wasn't all that was needed for a marriage, after all. There had to be some kind of compatibility.

Why hadn't she just told him she was pregnant, rather than approaching the subject obliquely? She should have come right out with it and let the chips fall where they might, instead of allowing him the opportunity to unwittingly say anything negative about the event.

Maybe it was her fault.

No, she decided. He didn't want children, and she hadn't burdened him with one.

Of course, she had finally relented and allowed him to pay for her to finish the year of schooling she needed. He'd called it pay for her year as his de facto assistant on the *Katharine*. She'd allowed him that much, not as a wife, but as an employee.

He wouldn't cooperate on a divorce, and Nicole hadn't pressed the issue because, in all the time since leaving him, she had never stopped loving the man. That was the worst part, the feeling that she couldn't stay with a man she so desperately loved.

As she finally fell asleep in her three-room rental just off-campus, her last thought was of David. He was what she had left undone.

THE MAN GLARED AT HER, his icy blue eyes piercing her from above the concealing mass of his beard. He was shouting, his words unheard above the gale of wind and water that roared around him. She sensed a great urgency in him, as though it were terribly important that she hear him. But she could hear nothing but the storm that washed her away from him and toward the rocky shore.

That was when she felt the rumbling of the ground beneath her and saw her possessions bouncing through the air once again.

And she woke up bathed in cold sweat, to sit upright, listening for any sound in the air. There was nothing, absolutely nothing. Not even the sound of crickets.

No crickets!

Suddenly compelled to action, Nicole flew from her bed and fumbled in terror with the knob of her door. Finally throwing the door open, she rushed across to Matthew's door and bounded through, just as the quake hit.

It grew from a slight vibration to a shivering roar as she snatched the still-slumbering child into her arms and ran to the door. The building seemed to be jumping on its foundations, knocking her to her knees, and she reached the relative safety of the door frame and knelt, huddling over the now screaming and thrashing infant.

She could hear her bed leaping in her room, accompanied by the crashing of her books and plants bouncing to the floor, just as they had in her dream.

She crouched lower, offering her own back as Matthew's shield, while the earth's angry rumbling grew around her. Pressing her eyes shut, barely breathing, she waited for the quake to pass.

But a crashing sound from the living room opened her eyes to stare through the swirling dust that filled the room, toward the door. A square of light from the hall pierced the gloom, the moving figure of a man interrupting it as he hurried toward her.

"Get out!" he cried as he ran toward her and her child.

Nicole cringed away from the stranger, but the strong hands that grasped her and urged her upward were too compelling to ignore. She hurried toward the door with the man, chasing the light in the hall toward safety, just seconds before the ceiling above the child's room gave way and the door frame that had been her shelter twisted and fell beneath the weight of the structure collapsing from above.

Chapter Two

Nicole faced David on the street before the remains of her apartment building, while Matthew settled into awed quiet as he watched the crowd of people forced out of the apartment building milling about them in confusion. Nicole and David stared at each other without speaking for a moment, winded by their flight from the collapsing structure.

"Thank God," he said at last. "I thought I'd be too late."

"David," Nicole answered. "Why are you here?" She was too shocked by the night's events to register anything beyond blank wonder at his sudden arrival.

"I had a dream. I was worried. Hell, Nicole, you're my wife," he said. "Of course I'm here. The problem is that I don't seem to have come soon enough," he added, staring in amazement at the child in Nicole's arms. "I don't imagine for a moment that you're baby-sitting or something, are you?"

"No, I..." What could she say to the father of her child, to explain the fact that she never told him? "I'm not baby-sitting," she said at last. "He's your son—Matthew."

"Why?" David could think of nothing else to say as he looked at the child squirming in Nicole's arms. "Why on earth didn't you tell me?"

"Why? You were the one who didn't want children!" she exclaimed. "Don't you try to tell me different now!"

"I didn't want— I didn't? That was the problem? Nicole, we sure could have worked something out about children. You left because of that?"

"You said it yourself, that you didn't want children!" Nicole said angrily.

"Christ, Nicole! You left because you were pregnant? Rather than just tell me, you took off? You owed it to me to tell me the truth."

"Owed it to you? Like a debt? I didn't owe you anything of the kind! I—"

Matthew began to cry in her arms just then, clinging to her as hot tears welled up in his clear blue eyes.

"Oh, look at this," Nicole said, softly, but with undimmed anger. "You've made him cry."

"*I* made him cry? I wasn't the only one shouting, Nicole," he said stubbornly. Then he stepped forward to place his hand atop his son's head. "His name is Matthew?"

"Yes, Matthew David."

"My grandfather's name," he said, smiling.

"And my favorite uncle's," she added pointedly.

"He's beautiful," David said softly, leaning closer to the youngster, who had ceased crying and was staring back at him solemnly. "This wasn't fair, Nicole."

"It's cold out here," she said, avoiding the subject in favor of their immediate problem. "We've got to get Matthew out of the cold."

"I have a cab," David said. "At least, I did have one." He turned then, noticing for the first time the number of people who were milling about on the street around them. His cab was still waiting for him.

Nicole marveled at the destruction around her. One side of her building had given way, four floors falling like a house of cards into the basement. Now it lay in a heap, half of the building down and half of it up but standing at a crazy angle. Burbles of water flowed up from the broken plumbing through the ruptured concrete to complete the destruction of the personal belongings remaining inside.

Across the street, flames smoldered in the wreckage of a ranch house that had succumbed to the quake, a crew of firemen spraying it with water while the displaced family watched in dull amazement.

Nicole made a quick inventory and noted that the only things she would want from inside her apartment were Matthew's baby book and the photograph album. Aside from her and Matthew's entire wardrobe, her small collection of books and her class notes, she really didn't have anything of value. She remembered that the baby book was wrapped in plastic in its original box, beneath her bed, so it was probably safe. And photographs could be dried out. As long as they hadn't been torn in the collapse of the building.

Her other things were replaceable. Now she looked around her, searching the faces in the small, dazed crowd for other residents of the building.

Fortunately, most of the inhabitants were college students, and it was a Friday night. There probably hadn't been anyone in her building who was sleeping besides herself, and she knew her neighbors well enough to know which of them would have been home at this time of night. It looked as though everyone were accounted for, by her tally. Thank God for that.

Gooseflesh stood up on her bare arms, and her nightgown, while quite opaque, and comfortable for sleeping, was no match for an ocean breeze at one in the morning. Matthew was comfortably encased in a sleeper that covered him from head to toe, but she was freezing. Nicole began wondering if someone in one of the untouched houses farther down the block might have a blanket to spare.

"Get us out of here," she said to David. She was too tired and cold to resist his help now.

"Let's go," he said. "Say, you're barefoot. Is that all you've got to wear?"

"I'm afraid so." A nightgown and a pair of panties was all she owned, and Matthew was wearing his only diaper beneath his sleeper.

"We'll get you some clothing in the morning," he said as he slipped out of his jacket and offered it to her. "Matt needs some diapers, too. We can pick them up on the way to the boat."

Nicole accepted his jacket and allowed him to take Matthew, who was nearly asleep again, from her. The child stirred and looked quizzically at David for a moment before nuzzling securely against his chest and slipping off to sleep again.

They walked away from the wreckage that held everything she owned and got into the waiting taxi. The neighborhoods through which they drove appeared to be untouched, though knots of people stood in the yards, talking and watching the glow of several fires to the north.

As they drove away, Matthew slumbering peacefully against Nicole's shoulder, she wasn't thinking of the ruin behind her, but of the uncertainty that lay ahead. The bearded wild man in her dream had become David, and now he had come to take her away.

She felt as though she had been abducted and hauled away in a cab to the marauder's ship. She and her son were his captives, for she was without any means of taking care of them without David.

Maybe this was what she had wanted all along. Maybe she had hoped he would come along and rescue her, regardless of her protests. She had certainly thought of it from time to time, and it had never been an entirely distasteful idea.

Sitting next to him now, both of them silent as the cab carried them through town to the docking facility at the beach, she felt the familiar warmth of her feelings toward him return in full measure. She loved this man, no matter their disagreements, and there was a sense of completion to being with him again. Even now, with David sitting in angry silence beside her, she felt her recent anxiety slipping away.

She felt, somehow, that she was home once more.

THEIR RETURN to David's ship seemed to proceed smoothly, in contrast to the chaos of sirens and rushing people around them. It was clear that David was planning on the two of them remaining together, now that fate had rejoined them, and Nicole didn't protest that assumption one bit. She had never really expected them to remain apart, after all, not in her heart. It was just that it had become increasingly hard to return as Matthew grew. For she couldn't help but feel that her position as the wronged party had been shifted to that of the person at fault, because she hadn't told him about his son.

David took the slumbering child from her at the pier, holding him gently, as though it were an entirely natural act for him.

"Let's get on the boat and get out of here." He was already hurrying along the pier toward the sailboat tied at the end of it.

"You're not planning to leave right away, are you? I can't go away now."

"Why not?" David said tersely. "You can't expect me to leave things as they are, can you?"

"No, but I've got my graduation."

"In a month."

"There's classes until then."

David sighed, patting his hand against the back of his son's head as the child stirred in his arms and rubbed one small fist against his eye. "All right," he said, "we'll talk about it in the morning."

They were nearing the boat now, and Nicole could see Jerry Brunsvold coming on deck in the illumination cast by the light at the end of the pier. A younger man emerged behind him. Jerry waved, smiling, as they hurried up the gangplank to the deck.

"God, David, you didn't have to kidnap her," he said. Then he laughed, slipping his arm around Nicole and kissing her cheek. "Welcome back, stranger. I see Captain Ahab found you all right."

"Hi, Jerry. Yes, he was there in the nick of time." It was easier to talk to Jerry than to David just then, and Nicole was glad for the sight of a friendly face.

"The emergency bands on the radio are full of activity," Jerry said. "Quite a nice little quake we happened onto."

"Are we fueled up?" David asked.

"Yes, all set," the other man said. He was blond, in his mid-twenties, and he regarded Nicole and Matthew with open curiosity. "New crew members?"

"My wife," David told him. "And this," he said, hoisting Matt around to hold him in both arms, "is my son, Matthew. Say hello to Ben Tucker," he told the child. "And this is your uncle Jerry."

"Hey, Matthew." Jerry laughed his greeting, holding both arms out to the boy. "Gimme," he said.

Nicole noted that David handed his son over without reluctance.

"I'll show you the ship," Jerry told Matt, bouncing the laughing child in his arms. "We'll have to put a leash on you, though, won't we?" he told his new friend. "You're way too young to go swimming." Then he turned to David, saying, more seriously, "I just spoke to home base. You better call."

"Okay. Ben, run ashore and buy a big box of diapers. There's an all-night store a couple blocks up. Two big boxes."

"I can go," Nicole offered.

"No," David said, sternly. "Say, Ben, if they have some kind of portable crib there, get that too."

"He's twenty-four pounds," Nicole said then, hurt by the brusque manner in which he had turned down her offer. "Any name brand is good."

"Right," David said, giving the young man money. "And I'll have to leave you or Paul ashore here. We need a cabin for the baby. You guys can draw straws, if you want."

"Cool," the crewman responded as he turned to walk along the pier, toward a market visible on the street at the end. David then turned to Nicole, lifting his arms as though to hug her, but letting them fall again.

"I'd better make that call," he said, and walked into the cabin.

"It looks like we're in for stormy seas," Jerry said, as much to Matthew as to her. "Well, you're here now, so I suppose that's a good sign."

She didn't know what to say to that, didn't know whether the signs were good or bad. But they did seem hopeful. "How has he been?" she asked instead, as they walked together into the cabin built into the deck of the sloop.

"How does he look?"

"Kind of shabby," she admitted.

"Well, that's how he's been."

She couldn't help notice a small note of accusation in Jerry's voice as he spoke just then, though it didn't seem directed entirely at her.

"Let's see what kind of sleeping arrangements we're going to have tonight," Jerry said. "This little swabbie needs to get back to bed-a-bye."

David was just finishing his conversation when Jerry led Nicole into the forward wheelhouse, and he replaced the receiver, a scowl darkening his square-cut features. He smiled, however, when he saw his son, and reached to take him from Jerry.

"Ever been on a sailing ship before, Buster?" he asked Matthew. "This is where we drive the boat. Tomorrow, maybe you can steer it."

Matthew cooed a response and tugged at David's beard, gleefully ignoring his surroundings.

"Matt, don't," Nicole said.

"That's all right." David laughed. "Maybe I have an excuse to shave now."

"I'm wondering where to bunk them," Jerry said. "You'd better get him back to bed, before he decides to stay up for the duration."

"Yes, well, I suppose Nicole can take our cabin," David said. "I'll bunk out here on the foldout."

Nicole said nothing about the arrangements, accepting their further separation as a matter of course. Neither of them could expect their marriage to just pop magically back together.

"If Ben doesn't find a crib, can Matt sleep in bed with you, Nicole?" David asked. "He won't roll out, will he?"

"He should be fine," she said. "I had better lock the door, though. Put a chair in front of it, maybe, so he doesn't get out of bed and wander off."

"He can walk?" David asked.

"Of course he can walk," she said. "He's fourteen months old, David."

"Okay. Jerry, we're going to have to buy something to enclose the guardrails. I don't suppose we can hold him twenty-four hours a day."

"No, you don't have to go to that trouble, David. We can't leave with you on the ship."

"Yes, you... Well, we can discuss that in the morning. It's been a big night, so let's all get some sleep." He turned and walked down the narrow corridor leading to his cabin, taking his son with him.

"He can't really expect us to just up and leave, can he?" Nicole asked Jerry.

"Leave it until morning," the man recommended. "Don't go running off in the middle of the night."

"I wasn't planning to," she said defensively. Anything further they might have said was cut off by Ben's arrival with diapers and a portable playpen.

NICOLE TURNED OUT the light and fell back on the bed immediately after she closed the cabin door. She let her body relax into the mattress, enjoying the feeling of being off her feet once again.

But she wasn't tired anymore, and she lay listening to the small sounds of the men moving on the ship, and the distant sounds of sirens and cars, nearly overwhelmed by the gentle lapping of the waves against the side of the ship.

This was his bed, their marriage bed, and it held the weight of memories within it. They had been so happy that first year, and all she could remember was the happiness, the all-consuming happiness, he'd given her. Those memories made their current situation all the harder to bear.

But the rocking of the boat and the murmur of the waves brought sleep to slip in past her worries and fears and dropped welcome darkness over her troubled thoughts.

DAVID SLEPT FITFULLY on the narrow bed in the wheelhouse as his dreams overwhelmed him. *She was holding him so tightly that he could barely breathe. Her breasts were pressed against him as their bodies rolled through the warm mist, united in love and urgent desire. Their movements built with aching slowness to the final release of so much frustrated yearning. His hands savored the supple warmth of her skin, moving hungrily over her as he sought to devour her with his lips. And the mist seemed to coil around them, warming and supporting them as they made love, until suddenly the mist was gone and he fell alone, with a violent jolt.*

To wake up alone aboard his gently bobbing ship, his need of her pressed painfully into the mattress. David clutched his pillow against his face and rolled onto his back wishing he could cry.

HE CARESSED HER THROAT lightly with his lips, moving lower still to tease each breast in turn, every touch bringing a new sparkle of sensation to the center of her womanhood as his lips tasted her and his fingers nimbly massaged her cares away. He rolled her onto her back, and she opened her legs to admit him, shuddering at their sudden union and the piercing . . .

... whine of a fire engine passing on the street near the dock, waking her abruptly from her sensuous dream.

Nicole rolled onto her side, tears rushing into the pillow.

"Oh, David," she whispered, "what have I done to our lives?"

Chapter Three

Nicole woke early to the sound of Matthew energetically rattling the frame of his playpen as he bounced himself against the mesh sides. She rolled over in the bed, taking a moment to remember why she felt her bed softly rocking beneath her. Then she stretched in the bed as she looked around the cabin at the woodwork, darkened by years of salt air, and the large, soft bed, bracketed by sunlit portholes, in which she lay. She smiled, feeling comfortable and rested. She felt at home.

Matthew noticed her wakefulness and shook his pen, shouting, "Ah-ma! Ah, ah!" and giggling.

"Okay, boss," Nicole said, sitting. "I'm up."

She stepped out of bed and lifted the child from his bed and laid him on hers to unzip his sleeper and get at his diaper. He was soaked, of course, and she changed him quickly and zipped the sleeper up again.

After taking care of her child, she opened David's closet and found his robe, to dress herself for an excursion on deck. Then she took Matt in her arms and left the cabin to greet the new day.

"Ya, ya, ya!" Matthew cried when he saw the ocean through the portholes of the ship's salon. He pointed excitedly, bouncing in Nicole's arms. "Ya! Ha, ah!"

"Yeah, right, kid, ya-ya," someone said.

Nicole turned quickly, finding a young man standing behind her smiling from the door to the galley. "Oh, hello," she said, rather startled.

"Hi. Sorry to surprise you," he said. "I'm Paul Gabriel, one of the galley slaves here on the *Bounty*."

"I'm Nicole Ellis," she replied, extending her hand to the dark-haired young man. "Nicole Ellis Germaine," she amended herself.

"Ben said you were aboard," the fellow said. "We've already drawn straws on who gets to stay ashore."

"I don't plan to put anyone out," she said, "but David seems to think I'm going with him."

"Aren't you?" he asked, his brown eyes probing her face earnestly as he stepped toward her, extending his hand.

"Not that I know of," she said, shaking his hand. "I've got school."

"Your passage seems to be booked already," Paul said somberly. "I'm all packed."

"Well, you can just unpack, then," she rejoined him. "I'll talk to David." She slung Matthew against her right hip and began walking forward, to the wheelhouse.

"The way things are going, it might be best that you go along, if he thinks it's important," the fellow called out behind her.

Nicole didn't stop to ask what he meant by that, but walked along the narrow hall running beside the cabins to the bright room where David and Jerry were standing at the wheel, looking over a nautical chart.

"Why are you kicking your crew off the boat?" she asked the two men. "I'm not going anywhere with you."

"Come on, Nicole, let's not get into it right off the bat," David said calmly. He smoothed one hand down over his beard as he turned toward her. "Things are happening too quickly to wait."

"Not even for an explanation? What things are you talking about?"

"Lots of things, none of them good. I've got trouble, and you're involved, whether you like it or not. Sit down," he suggested. "This may take a couple cups of coffee to explain."

"I'm going to check the galley," Jerry said, diplomatically, leaving the room.

"Fine, but if I feel this ship moving while you're explaining, I'm out of here," she warned him as she slipped in behind the small table and placed Matthew on the vinyl bench beside her.

"We're not going anywhere yet," he assured her as he brought two cups of coffee to the table and sat on a canvas chair across from her. He paused for a moment, watching Matthew turn around on his knees on the bench and stand uncertainly to slap his hand against the chart tacked to the cork bulletin board above the bench.

"It starts in Australia," David said at last. "I mapped a new quadrant there. Not on *our* trip, but on the return last year," he added, referring to their working honeymoon, spent sailing through the South Pacific. "We got a strange reading near the Tonga Trench, north of New Zealand, so we did a detail of the ocean floor in that area. It turned out that the reading was coming from an observation satellite that had gone down after an aborted launch last year. I was picking up an electrical signal from the satellite's batteries."

"Observation satellite?"

"Spy satellite." He sipped his coffee, grimacing at the taste. "We reported its location, in general terms, and let it go at that. I didn't think it mattered much, and the Department of Defense didn't care where it was, as long as it was under about four and a half miles of water. It wasn't any good to them anymore, since the salt water would have ruined the circuits anyway."

"What's that got to do with our sailing with you?" she asked skeptically.

"Hang on to your hat, Nicole," he said. "I'm getting there." Then he leaned forward to pat Matthew on the back, saying, "Hey, watch it, sport. Nicole, he's going to get that pushpin out in another second."

Nicole took her son away from the map, where he had been busily wiggling one of the pins holding it in place. "Owie thing," she told the child. "No, no, owie thing."

"There are a lot of owie things on board, Nicole," David said.

"I'm aware of that," she said defensively. "I've got him under control. Just get on with your story." She cuddled the young boy to her chest and looked quickly around the cabin at the many sharp or heavy things that were within his young grasp.

"Okay, so I hadn't given the matter much thought until I was contacted by a fellow wanting to buy directions to the location of the satellite, and, if possible, my services to salvage it."

"Somebody wants a broken satellite?"

"Yeah, and they wanted me to get it for them. I turned him down, of course. He made me a better offer, which I turned down, too, and that was the end of it, until a month ago. The request was made once more, a bit more forcefully. They blew up my Jaguar in New Jersey."

"What? Are you sure of that?"

"Positive. Not a big flashy explosion, mind you. It looked like an engine fire, but I got a phone call after it happened, explaining it to me, so I wouldn't miss the point."

"And you're saying that someone blew up your car because of a satellite that isn't any good anyway?" Her heart leapt at the news of the trouble David found himself in, but she was skeptical nonetheless. It didn't make any sense to her.

"It's not working anymore," he said. "But it is intact. I've got videotape of the satellite, showing the nose cone still in place over most of it. Apparently, when they aborted the launch and blew up the rocket, the nose cone blew free in the explosion. The payload was supposed to be destroyed, but wasn't."

"So what?"

"If they get the satellite, they can take it apart and replicate it through reverse engineering. More importantly, the program chips are encased in a sealed section of the satellite, and should be protected from the salt water for another year. See, the battery is still functioning, so that means the chips are still dry."

"It seems like a lot of work to go through for some chips," Nicole commented.

"Chips worth millions—maybe billions—of dollars," David reminded her. "And that's just for the design of the chips themselves. The information in the program is top secret."

"Just who is this person wanting all this? Turn him in to the authorities."

"His name is Morley Kraft," David said seriously. "Believe me, I tried to report him. The trouble is, I have no proof. The cops won't listen, and the Department of Defense doesn't really care, since the cold war has ended and we don't have any enemies in any position to use the chips against us at the moment. Besides, not many people are equipped to bring up the satellite. It's down a little over twenty thousand feet."

"But Morely Kraft thinks he can get you to do it."

"He's sure trying hard. In fact, our office in New Jersey had a small fire overnight," David told her.

"My goodness, David, was anyone hurt?"

"No, thank God, and nothing was badly damaged, but it was clearly arson. He wants me to know he can hurt us badly if he wants to."

"What does any of this have to do with me?"

"Everything. He can destroy my property, but if he proves to be a threat against you, he's got me. He knows that, and that's why we looped up here after starting out on a very different course. I had to get to you without letting him know I was coming, for fear that I'd force his hand. I knew you were safe so far, but I just couldn't be sure how long that safety would last."

Nicole looked out the porthole at the calm ocean beyond the boat. It was hard to think that so sinister a conspiracy could exist along with the azure sky and the tranquil blue sea, and the good-natured squirming of her son in her arms made it doubly hard to imagine such evil.

"Who is Morley Kraft?" she asked him then.

"He's an Australian millionaire who overextended himself in the eighties and is facing bankruptcy now," David replied. "He invested far too extensively in wool, just before the market went to hell and Australia hit the recession along with most of the rest of the world. The last profitable venture he has going is in the arms trade, so it's natural for him to want the satellite. He's got the connections to sell the technology."

"Just because he's a big shot doesn't mean he's above the law," Nicole said. "Surely someone in the government would be willing to at least check the story out."

"I'll sure give them a chance," he said. "But not before I'm sure that you're safe and sound. It'll take them time to check things. Besides, he's had several U.S. government contracts over the years, and he owes big money to several U.S. banks, so the tendency will be to lean toward believing Kraft.''

"Oh, David, you're making this into quite a conspiracy, aren't you?''

"No conspiracy, just good business,'' he replied. "If he goes to jail before he gets his affairs in order, his creditors will only get about ten cents on the dollar. That fact gives him about two hundred million dollars' worth of insulation. And it takes time to cut through all of that.''

"But it's not realistic to shanghai me and Matthew until it's all settled. I'm only a month away from my degree.''

"If you'd let me help, I could probably get you some slack in that department,'' David said. "If Morley Kraft's money can keep him out of jail, then I should think a bit of my money should be able to help you graduate law school.''

"No way!'' Nicole exclaimed. "I'm not buying a degree!''

"Who said you would be? You've done the work, so it's stupid to have to put off your graduation until the end of the fall quarter because circumstances forced you to leave early. You wouldn't be buying anything but a midsummer makeup test and the delivery of your diploma.''

"That doesn't matter. I'm not going to start tossing your money around now.''

"Okay,'' he said. "I'll butt out. Just keep it in mind.''

"I won't,'' she insisted. "I've already forgotten you offered.''

"In that case, I guess you'll just have to take a short break from your studies to cruise with me," he said, clearly unwilling to take no for an answer. "I should spend some time with my son, anyway."

"Don't you go using Matthew to make me feel guilty," Nicole warned.

"I'm not. I'm trying to use him to make you want to be safe. Put your career on hold for a month and keep him from harm, okay?"

"I think we're in more danger with you than without you," she said. "Have you thought of that?"

"Yes, I have thought of that," he admitted. "And I don't think it's true. They can't pressure me into anything by threatening to harm me, because they need me. They can only get to me by threatening the people I love. I'd rather have you where I can keep an eye on you. Especially now," he added, when she began to continue her protest, "when I know I've got a son to be worried about. Especially now."

"You're going to play the big daddy role for all it's worth now, aren't you?" Nicole said, angry both at him for his presumption and at herself for her secrecy about their son. "You were adamant about not wanting children before, David. They would tie you down and hamper your research, wouldn't they? That's what you said. I'd hate to tie you down."

"No matter what I may have said," David replied evenly, with an obvious effort to control his voice, "and no matter what I think now, you and Matthew are my responsibility. I can't shirk that."

"Responsibility? God, what century are we living in?" Nicole glared at him, keeping her voice to a harsh whisper, in deference to the child in her arms. "I am my own responsibility, and Matthew is my responsibility. I've taken the responsibility, and if I had wanted to rely on you, I would have asked for your help!"

"Nonetheless, it's my trouble that endangers you, Nicole, so you must admit that it is my responsibility to shelter you from that much, at least."

"So hire a guard for us and go away," Nicole spit out. "I've got classes to finish and tests to take. I can't go anywhere now."

"Sorry, but I'm not going to leave my wife and son in danger, and that's all there is to it." David stood up, a slight smile flickering at the corners of his expressive lips. "Come on, dear, relax and take a little cruise. It won't be so bad."

"But a child on board your precious boat? How could you possibly stand that?" Nicole asked archly. "We don't want to put you out."

"Morley Kraft has already put me out, Nicole. But he did me a service, too. He gave me an excuse to come for you. Morley Kraft allowed me to find out about my son, when my own wife wanted to keep him from me."

David turned and left the cabin before she could reply, leaving her feeling a growing sense of anger and frustration. She had been wrong to withhold the knowledge of Matthew's birth, but he was wrong to take this commanding tone with her. She didn't feel that she was in any danger, and she thought his whole attitude was a grandstand play. Responsibility? If he had wanted the responsibility, he would have had it two years ago, when she first found out she was pregnant! No, he hadn't wanted the responsibility of a child then, and he was only using the word to make himself look big now.

"Your father is a pigheaded fool," she said to Matthew, nuzzling her face against his blond hair. "I just wish I knew if he was right or not."

The sound of footsteps on the wooden deck brought her attention back to the entrance to the cabin. Jerry Brunsvold stepped through, smiling.

"There's an empty cabin for you now, Nicole," he said. "We can sail any time."

"This is foolish," she told him. "I'm in no danger."

"Maybe not," he admitted as he sat across from her at the narrow table. "But the odds are stacked against you. Statistically, anyway, David is being prudent by insisting that you come with us. Of course, the safest bet of all would be protective custody away from him, too."

"What, a jail cell?"

"No, a nice hotel suite someplace, with twenty-four-hour guards. I suggested that, but he didn't figure you'd like that any better."

"No, I wouldn't."

"I wouldn't, either. And now, well, I don't suppose David will be very eager to let this little guy out of his sight." Jerry leaned forward, reaching to tousle Matthew's hair.

"Oh, sure, he's the proud papa, isn't he? He doesn't even like children."

"You didn't give him much of a chance," Jerry said.

"I was told often enough how children would interfere with his plans," Nicole said, scoffing.

"David made some arrangements about your school," Jerry said, changing the subject diplomatically. "You can't take any tests off-campus, but they'll allow you to write any final papers and fax them in to your professors. We're equipped for that right here."

"I didn't ask anyone to make arrangements."

"Lighten up a bit, will you? He knows this is a hardship for you, and he's doing what he can to make it easier."

"Oh, I suppose he is," she admitted, "but that doesn't make me any happier about it. This whole thing is so ludicrous."

"Not as bad as it might have been. He wanted to go after you and drag you back right away."

"But he didn't, did he?"

"You were very clear about not wanting him to, Nicole. After about the fiftieth time you told him to leave you alone, he started to believe you."

Nicole took a deep breath and let it out slowly, pondering her situation. It was obvious that she wasn't going to get off the ship, no matter what she said or did. She wasn't sure she wanted to, either. After all, if there was a danger to her son, it would make sense to keep him surrounded by people working to guard him. The idea of danger seemed impossible on such a beautiful day, but David believed in it. Though David might use the possibility of harm to Matthew as a ploy to keep her on the ship, Jerry wouldn't. It was clear that he believed in the danger from the Australian tycoon just as much as David did.

"Okay," she said at last. "I won't jump ship."

"Good." Jerry smiled. "Meanwhile, we will try to figure out a way to get Morley Kraft off our backs, so you can go back to your lawyering."

"Is he really that much of a threat?"

"I'd say so. He can buy all the help he needs. If we had some concrete proof against him, we'd be all right, but we'll never get that."

"So what can you do?"

"I think we should salvage the satellite, just like he wants us to," Jerry said.

"You can't do that!" Nicole insisted.

"You too? That's what David said, but I figure there are a lot of ways to ruin the chip on the way up from the bottom. It's down awfully deep, after all. Besides, if we actually go after it, we might be able to get the Department of Defense to take an interest in us."

"And they'll arrest you along with Kraft when you bring it up."

"Probably."

"You'll have to do something. It sounds as if this guy will be after you forever."

"No, I'd guess the seawater will be able to get through the casing to short out the batteries within a year. That will fry the chip. And Kraft's finances and legal state are bad enough now that he'll either be bankrupt or indicted before then. He needs it now or never."

"Say, if this guy has been after you about it for a month or more, why did David suddenly decide that I was in danger, too?" The delay seemed bothersome to

Nicole, for if David had been that terribly concerned, she would have expected him to come sooner.

"We thought it would be best to stay away from you," Jerry said. "But we changed plans after we rounded Tierra del Fuego on our way to the South Pacific."

"Why then?"

"I don't really know for certain." Jerry smiled. "But David said he had a dream that you were in danger, so we changed course."

"A dream?" The thought chilled Nicole just then. She had been dreaming, too, and her dream had come to life in the earthquake.

"Yes," Jerry said, voicing her thoughts perfectly. "And we got here just in time for your earthquake, didn't we?"

Chapter Four

I don't know what I'd do with children right now, Nicole. I mean, they're cute and all that, but they do get underfoot, and they wreak havoc with a person's work schedule. I just can't help but think that kids would be more work than they're worth.

David's words rang in Nicole's ears as she took a cab back to her apartment that morning. He'd said them two years ago, those and other words, but they still had a hurtful immediacy in Nicole's heart. She could still feel their sting.

What good was honesty if all it could do was hurt?

But that didn't matter now, did it? They'd had their fight, and she'd run from the knowledge that he wouldn't welcome the child that grew within her. She'd run and kept him away for over two years—until now.

Now was what mattered. Now was when she must pay for her deceit and he must reevaluate his words and feelings. There was no turning back now. He could no more pretend that he had no child than she could pretend she had no husband.

And she could no longer even try to tell herself that she didn't love him; she knew better than that, now that he was near once more.

The city hadn't suffered very terribly at the hands of nature last night. According to the news reports and her cabby, the quake had been a mild one and the damage was primarily concentrated along her block and a couple farther north. Her building was old, built before the stronger California codes, and so had taken the most damage.

For the most part, however, the only real signs of the quake were in the slight tilt of street signs and light poles, and the few new cracks in the sidewalks along the way. People were out on the streets, just as though nothing had happened, going about the business of their lives.

Her cab could proceed no farther than the police barricade at the end of her block, waiting for her while she walked to the remains of her building to retrieve her belongings.

One side of her building had collapsed to lie in a tilted heap piled on the first floor. The lawn was damp, but the water had been shut off and no longer flowed from the broken plumbing inside.

Nicole approached her building carefully, trying to recognize something in the crushed half that might tell her where the remains of her apartment lay amid the rest. Then she saw it, a bit of curtain hanging in a triangle of window frame, visible only about five feet above ground level and easily accessible over the slabs of broken concrete. That was her bedroom curtain!

And it looked as though there were space to crawl inside the room through the window.

Hurrying to the building before someone could spot her and stop her, Nicole climbed up and knelt and peered inside the tumble of concrete and brick that had been her home. Yes, she could see her floor tilting away from her, and her bed still mostly in place by the window. Now, if she could reach beneath it, she might be able to retrieve Matthew's baby book and photo album, and the videotape she'd made of him at various points in his young life.

She grasped the edge of the window, checking for glass, and then, when nothing rumbled or cracked at the pressure, she leaned inside.

It was a tight squeeze, even for someone of her lithe figure, but she managed to slip through the window into the slightly larger space of the room. The ceiling brushed her head, and dust fell around her in a cloud that made her cough, but she snaked farther in and reached beneath the bed, which was still standing on its legs.

Yes, she could feel the plastic K mart bag in which she'd kept the books and tape, and she thanked God she hadn't gotten around to clearing a space on a bookshelf for these precious items.

The bag stuck slightly, giving her a momentary fear that the contents might be crushed, but it came free with a forceful tug, and she pulled it to her and felt inside in the darkness to be certain that everything was still inside. It seemed that everything was there. Now all she had to do was to get out again.

There was no room to turn, so she had to slither backward, feeling with her feet for the opening through which she'd entered. It seemed to take forever to get the lower half of her body out of the building, and the creaking sounds the rubble was making grew ominously with each movement. A loud snap stopped her movement as the floor beneath her shook, and she lay, barely breathing, with her toes just touching the grass outside, until she dared move once more.

"'Ello," someone called outside, the word clipped off by his accent. "Use a 'and, can you?"

"No, I'm fine," Nicole said, pushing herself backward once more. But the space seemed to have narrowed a bit, and it was harder getting out than in.

"No worry, miss," the man said. "I'll give you a 'and."

He touched her legs at the knees, his hands sliding halfway up her thighs and grasping and pulling lightly. When she'd come out a bit more, he slipped his hands to her hips, staying in contact in an intrusive manner. He slipped his arms around her waist and pulled once more as she pushed herself out of the window frame.

Nicole came gratefully into the light and stood as the man continued holding her, his arms moving upward now, hands brushing over her breasts as he pressed his body against her back, his face brushing in over her shoulder, his cheek to her cheek.

"There you go," he whispered, "safe and sound, aren't you?"

"Let go of me," she said quietly, fear seeping into her like cold water. The man had an Australian accent.

"You're safe as houses, aren't you?" He laughed, tightening his grip. One hand moved up to her throat, touching her lightly, while the other moved on her chest. "Some houses, anyway."

"What do you want?" His hand on her breast told her the worst, his tobacco breath in her face warned her of the worst. But this was daylight!

"What you got there?" he asked. "You went in after some bloody books?"

"A baby book," she whispered.

"Ah, that would be young Matthew, then. Right?"

"How do you know?"

"Oh, you may lie to your husband, but you can't keep secrets from someone who won't respect your privacy," he whispered. "We know. Tell your hubby to be a good boy," he said then. "Tell him we're still willing to pay for his efforts."

Then he released her, stepping back as she turned to face him, backing away, clutching her bag to her chest. It was the blond man she'd seen on campus, the one she had thought was watching her but could never be sure. He was smiling now, his teeth a glaring white in the dark, tanned mask of his face.

Nicole turned and ran.

"YOU LET HER leave the ship?" David stared angrily at Jerry, paying no attention to the child in his arms, who was tugging happily at his hair.

"She's not going to run away, David," Jerry assured him. "She said that she had to get something from the house if she could, and that she would be right back."

"She didn't even have clothing to wear."

"Sure she did. You packed up that box of her jeans and blouses, remember? She'll be right back."

"I don't like this one bit." David left the cabin and hurried onto the deck, looking anxiously across the wharf toward the town. "I'd better go after her," he said, and began walking down the gangplank to the dock.

"Hey, Papa," Jerry called out. "Don't you think you should leave Junior behind?"

"What? Oh, yes. I guess I'm getting ahead of myself."

David walked back on deck and stood looking at his son in his arms. "I have to call a cab, anyway," he said. "What's wrong with your mother, Matthew? Has she no sense at all?"

"She'll be fine," Jerry assured him.

"Probably." But the worry lingered in David's voice, and his eyes were narrowed in concern. Still, he managed a smile when he looked at his son. "He's sure a good-looking kid, isn't he? Got his mother's nose."

"A fine boy," Jerry agreed. "Got your eyebrows."

"You think so?" David grinned broadly. "You're a cutie, aren't you?" he said, tickling the child's stomach. "A cute little dickens, you are."

Matthew laughed loudly, throwing his head back and tugging at David's hair.

"Ouch!" David knelt to balance Matthew on his knee and disentangle his fingers from his hair. "I've got to get my hair cut."

"And it's about time, too." Then Jerry stepped forward, looking ashore. "Here's a cab now," he said.

David stood with Matthew, following Jerry's gaze to the approaching vehicle.

The cab stopped, and its rear door flew open and Nicole rushed up the gangplank to the boat.

"Cast off," she exclaimed, carrying a plastic-wrapped bundle onto the boat with her. "Let's get out of here!"

"What changed your mind so suddenly?"

"Your Australian friend is in town. He was at the apartment. He was very good at convincing me."

"Who?" David rushed to her, reaching instinctively to grasp her shoulder. "Did he hurt you?"

"No, he just scared the hell out of me."

David turned, still holding Matthew, and shouted, "Come on, Ben, cast off! Crank her up, Jerry, we're out of here!"

Nicole took Matthew and stood trembling as she watched the men prepare the sailing vessel. Her journey from the destroyed apartment building had done little to steady her nerves. If anything, she was more anxious now, with her son in her arms, than she had been when it was just her own safety at stake. The thought of that vicious man being able to do anything to this precious baby was horrifying to Nicole, and the only steadying influence she had right now was the sight of David moving with urgency to take them away from the threat. Still, Nicole didn't feel that they could ever be safe from that man, even at sea.

He had made certain that she knew he would stop at nothing to achieve his goal. No, nothing was sacred to a man like that, and no one was safe from him.

How could they stop such determination? If David was right about him—and she had no reason to doubt him now—the Australian was practically invulnerable to any legal restraints. Lacking any concrete evidence, they could do little to prove any claims against him. So what could they do?

It was strange for Nicole to be at a loss for a plan of action in any situation. She was normally a decisive woman, but at the moment she felt bullied into stupidity.

"Hey, Paul!" David shouted into the main cabin. "Get in gear, buddy, we're taking off!" Then he turned to Ben Tucker, who was standing in the stern, and shouted, "All clear?" Then, to the wheelhouse: "Okay, Jerry, put it in gear! Paul! Get off the boat!"

Paul Gabriel emerged from the cabin, laden with a suitcase and duffel bag. "Okay, I'm off," he called out, running toward the gangplank still standing against the ship. "You guys, don't lose my CDs. I didn't have time to get them."

"Just so long as you remember which ones are yours," Ben replied, running to push the plank away as soon as his crewmate ran down to the dock.

"Happy cruising!" Paul put his bags down on the dock and took the gangplank from Ben and laid it aside on the dock. "I'll be here on the beach, working on my tan."

"Lucky stiff!"

"You got your pay?" David hurried toward them as the ship began to pull away.

"And a bonus!" the smiling lad replied.

"Who paid you a bonus?" David asked.

"Bye-bye!" Paul waved. "Bye, Matthew, catch you on the return trip!"

Matthew recognized his name and looked around for the source, and Nicole held him tighter to her bosom, vowing to protect him from all future menace. This small bundle of life was more important to her than her own, and far more vulnerable, as well.

Nicole watched the preparations with increased trepidation. She almost laughed at the thought that a day ago her worst worry had been a bad grade in corporate law.

FROM THE DOCK, Paul Gabriel watched the ship slip out to sea, picking up speed as it left him behind on the shore. Late spring in California wasn't the worst time of year to be released from his duties on the ship for a while. He pondered his next move with a happy heart.

Maybe he'd get a hotel room and see what was happening here, or maybe move down the coast a bit. Malibu sounded good, and it was good to be young and unfettered by responsibility in the summer. He left the dock whistling quietly and smiling at the odd feeling of firm ground beneath his feet. He was too used to the rolling deck to become quickly accustomed to footing that held still beneath him.

Passing a restaurant near the docks, Paul caught a glimpse of a man seated at a table near the front window. A blond fellow dressed in a tan shirt and slacks, he seemed awfully familiar. When he turned to look at the man again, however, he was gone. No matter, the guy probably just looked like some actor in a movie he'd seen. Paul Gabriel didn't know anyone in Carmel.

Still, the brief glimpse of the face he'd seen stuck with him, tugging at his memory as he walked along toward a Holiday Inn sign up the street. He had seen that face before, but where?

The sidewalk was empty before him, the few storefronts were devoid of people at the moment, and Paul continued walking toward the hotel with his duffel over his shoulder and his suitcase weighing down his other arm. The sound of a man's scuffling footsteps behind him made him stop then, and he turned and saw the blond man approaching quickly.

"Hey, fella," the man said, "I thought you'd be shipboard for this."

"What?" He turned, almost recognizing the man. "What do you mean?"

"We can't pick it up without your help with the equipment," he said. "A few coordinates aren't enough."

"I don't know what you're talking about," Paul said. "Who are you?"

"Oh." A look of consternation passed over the blond man's puglike features. "Sure, you're the other one, aren't you?"

"Other what?"

"Too bad, buddy," the man said, glancing around furtively. "My mistake, your injury."

Paul heard the clicking sound of a switchblade opening without knowing what it was, and when the man drove the knife into his stomach, he thought at first that the fellow had punched him. A second later, a piercing hotness proclaimed the nature of his injury as the man pulled upward, lifting him slightly. And then someone called out, and Paul's assailant withdrew his knife and ran.

Paul Gabriel stood for a moment, still holding his suitcase and duffel bag. Then his hands released their burdens and sought to stop the numbing pain growing outward from his abdomen. He stared at the crimson stain on his shirt for a moment, took a single step, collapsed to his knees and then fell flat on the pavement as a crowd began to gather around him.

Just before darkness overcame him, he remembered where he'd seen the face before.

Chapter Five

David watched his son playing on the floor of the main salon of the ship. They weren't equipped with toys, but the child was making fine use of a variety of utensils from the galley, busily clanging a wooden spoon around in a pan.

Such small, delicate fingers he had. His small face bore a look of concentration as he made his music on the floor. Tiny bare feet; beautifully formed toes. David watched him with a lump growing in his throat.

My God, that's my son!

If he had known, had had any idea about Matthew... but he hadn't had a clue. He had thought the worst pain he would have to endure by letting Nicole have the privacy she apparently wanted was his own separation from her. But that pain was nothimg compared to what he felt at this moment.

Was this his punishment for his unthinking remarks about not wanting children? Was this empty longing for the time he'd missed his torment for being a fool? He hadn't had any time to adjust to the idea of a child or to learn how wonderful the birth of his son might be. And now he felt a weight on his shoulders for every moment of his son's life that he had missed.

Life was cruel.

He sat for twenty minutes watching Matthew play. He wanted to pick him up, but wanted to just sit and watch as well. David wanted everything at once, the touch, the sound, the smell, the total presence of this child. His child. The sight of his son at play was miraculously wonderful.

Matthew's first steps, his first words and his first tooth were all history now. He might read about it in Matthew's baby book, like a student learning about an ancient civilization, but he could never experience it for himself.

Feeling as he did, he could almost hate Nicole for what she had done. Almost, but not really. No, it was his fault, for having been so insensitive.

A small sound from the hall alerted him to a new presence in the room, and he turned his head away from Matthew's activities to look at Nicole, who stood watching him from the door. Nicole, his beautiful wife, was back aboard ship, where she belonged.

She stood hesitantly, not knowing whether she should enter the cabin or not. Her son and husband looked ... perfect. That was all she could really think, that they looked perfect together, even though there was a distance between them still. It was as though David weren't sure if he should touch the child or not.

It was horrible, really. That she could have kept them apart, no matter what the reason, was a crime.

"Come in," David said. "There's no sense hanging around in the hall."

"I was afraid I might interrupt some male bonding," she said awkwardly.

"I'm just watching him to make sure he didn't crawl out on deck."

David didn't know what to say. Any statement of the love he had for the child now might seem like a reflection of anger at her for leaving him as she had. He didn't want to reproach her or argue, for he felt she was somewhat justified. He remembered the arguments before she'd left. He remembered what he'd said without ever considering that there might be a special reason for her tenderness on the subject of children. He had behaved like a fool.

"You can pick him up, if you want to," she said.

"Oh, yeah, I know," he said. "I'm just watching him play. He's very creative. If he gets tired of the pots and pans, I'll pick him up and let him pull my hair for a while."

"He seems to like doing that."

Nicole looked at her son, who had paused to regard her for a moment before returning to his task of stacking a pan and several plastic bowls into a tower. His little body swayed easily with the gentle rocking motion of the boat, and he didn't even seem to notice the movement; he was a sailor already.

"You do look a bit wild," Nicole said, walking into the cabin and brushing her fingers lightly against the hair that cascaded past her husband's shoulders. "Could use a trim."

"I don't know if I even have a razor anymore," David said, scrubbing his fingers through the thick beard that hid the lower portion of his face. He laughed. "The trouble with beards is that once you've gotten past the itching stage and it grows in nice and thick, you find you'd rather not bother with shaving again."

"I could give you a hand," Nicole offered. "You've got a scissors, haven't you?"

"Sure, but you're not a licensed barber, are you?"

"Come on, David, I can't possibly make you look any worse."

"Hey!" he said with a laugh, standing. "I thought I looked rather nautical."

"Maybe, but Captain Ahab was not a sympathetic character. Come on and get the scissors. Let's play barbershop."

David walked to the galley and got a scissors and a towel, pausing for a moment to watch the sea outside. They were making good time moving south along the California coast, with the engines chugging along at full throttle. There wasn't enough wind for them to use the sails, and with Paul ashore they were shorthanded, so they were relying on the "stinkpots," as sailors called marine engines. Wherever they were going, they were making good time at it.

He wasn't sure what his plan was, but whatever it was, having a child to care for complicated it immensely. Maybe Jerry was right, and what he ought to do is to retrieve the satellite and hope to sabotage it in the process.

He took the scissors back and handed them to his wife.

My wife. This is my wife.

Their marriage seemed new again, for it had been so long since he'd felt anything but pain in their relationship.

This is my wife. This is my child. My family.

He sat and let Nicole wrap the towel around him while Matthew watched from the floor.

"Just don't move," she warned him. "I don't want any accidents."

"I trust you with sharp utensils," he joked.

She trimmed his beard down deftly, revealing his strong jaw as she snipped it down to about an inch and then shorter, leaving an irregular stubble through which her husband's skin shone white. How long had it been since the sun had touched that flesh?

She used the scissors to cut his hair to a reasonable distance above his collar in back, and then began trying to shape the sides.

"I don't know how this is going to look," she warned him. "As you pointed out, I'm not really a barber."

"Anything will do, really," he said. "I'm not planning to pose for any pictures. You should probably leave a bit on my neck, or I'm going to get one hell of a sunburn."

"Oops." It was already too late to leave any cover for the pale skin of his neck. "I hope you've got sunscreen."

"I think Ben does." David paused a moment, reluctant to broach an upsetting subject. "You never explained exactly what happened at the apartment," he said. The slight shiver that went through her fingers at the question gave him more of an answer than he had expected to receive.

"I'd rather not dwell on it," she said tightly. But they were safe now, weren't they? And he really ought to know everything, shouldn't he? Nicole felt that it was foolish to be so frightened after the fact, but that didn't change how she felt about it.

"What exactly did the guy look like?"

"He was blond," she answered. "Australian accent. He was dressed in tan pants and one of those safari-type shirts."

"Wavy hair? Slicked back?"

"Yes, do you know him?"

"Garth Donnelly," David said. "I've never met him, but it sounds like him."

"How do you know?"

"I made a few calls and got some pictures and background on the people Kraft would most likely use for extortion of this sort. Donnelly would be at the top of the list. What did he do?"

"Threatened me and Matthew if we didn't get you to help them out. He made the threat sound as nasty as he could."

David sat in silence for a moment, imagining how the man might have managed to scare a strong woman like Nicole. The thoughts made him angry, and gave him a feeling of helplessness that he didn't like.

"I'm sorry you had to go through that, Nicole," he said at last. "But I'll see to it that it doesn't happen again."

"So, what's the plan?" she asked, happy to move on to any other topic, as she continued working on his coiffure.

"I think that when we get to New York I'll get in touch with Morley Kraft and agree to do the job for him. It's really the best bet. He's not going to do anything that will hold up in court or make any moves that will trap him. Jerry has an idea that maybe we can do something to ruin the thing on the way up. Expose the chips to seawater, or something."

"Yes, you could try that," Nicole agreed, "but he'd still have the hardware, so he could make a copy, wouldn't he?"

"The program is what he wants most. He can copy and sell that, with little cost or effort on his part. Reverse-engineering the hardware would take quite some time. Besides, once he's got the thing in hand, we'll have evidence."

"I guess so. But once he's got the satellite, what would keep him from sinking the *Katharine,* with all hands aboard her? It's obvious he'll stop at nothing." A shudder swept through her as she remembered the man at her apartment building. No, he wouldn't flinch at killing all of them. "I don't think it's a smart idea to pick up that satellite, David," she warned him.

"No, it's not a smart idea, but it may be the only idea I've got. I'll admit that I don't know what to do."

She worked in silence for a moment, enjoying the fleeting touches necessitated by her role as makeshift barber. The nuances of their remembered lovemaking, the small touches and lingering kisses, flashed through her mind.

"Well, at least we're safe for now," she said, her mouth suddenly dry at his nearness.

"Yes, we're safe," he said.

It pained him to realize how awkward he felt talking to his own wife, as though she were an acquaintance, rather than the most intimately known person in his life. He knew and loved every inch of her body, yet they were acting like strangers, when he longed to sweep her up in his arms and carry her to his cabin. It had been so long—too long.

"That's one hell of a kid we've got there," he said haltingly.

Matthew had stopped clattering his pans and bowl around and was sitting watching his mother transform the hairy stranger he'd first met into an entirely different person.

"He's quite inventive," David said.

"Yes, that's for sure. It never fails—if someone buys him a toy, he always seems to have more fun playing with the box it came in than the toy itself."

David couldn't speak for a moment. The thought of his son receiving toys, gifts, made him think of birthdays and Christmases, and the time he had lost. Family times that he had missed. For a moment, he felt a renewed surge of anger toward her.

"You should have told me," he said, before he had time to think about his words.

"You should have wanted children," she said.

But I do, he thought. *I really do.*

Still, he said nothing, sitting in stony silence while equal parts love, anger and regret warred within his heart. He felt sad and defeated.

Nicole sensed the tension in him, felt his neck muscles taut beneath her hand as she trimmed a bit more hair away. She wanted to bend slightly to kiss his neck and slip her hands around to stroke his broad chest once more. She longed to feel those arms around her, the hands that gripped the arms of his chair caressing her body. God, how she longed for his touch.

It had been too long since they'd been together as husband and wife.

But, even if they had both felt free to give in to such notions, their son was watching them, depending on them to protect him from the dangers of the sea. He was their responsibility, their charge to guide through life.

Matthew stood and toddled uncertainly to grab David's knee, cocking his head to stare up at his shaggy face. "Agah boo?" he asked. "Mama?"

"Yes, Matt, this is the same man you were assaulting earlier," she assured her son. "This is Daddy."

"Da," he said, trying the sound on for size. "Da," he repeated, liking the noise it made. He pulled at the leg of David's trousers, giving the unmistakable signal that he wanted to be picked up.

"I don't know," David said. "Your mother isn't very proficient with those scissors. Maybe you don't want to be up here just yet."

"I'm finished." Nicole stepped back. "And I think I did a darn good job of making a respectable man out of you."

"Wait till I shave, and we'll see," he said. He turned a bit to remove the towel and brush some of the hair away from his shirt, then picked up his son in his arms and held him so that the child could get a good look at him without the beard.

"Ooooh," Matthew said. He placed his small hands on both of his father's cheeks and patted him. "Oooooh! Ya!" When he tried in vain to get a grip on his father's formerly long beard, he satisfied himself with stroking the stubble and laughing.

"Is it that bad? I'm not going to pay for the haircut, if that's the kind of reception it gets in society."

"I know, you'd rather be a shaggy bear, and your son would rather have a beard to pull, but I think he'd be better off getting to know his father properly. You don't want to leave him with Captain Ahab as his first image of Daddy."

But each mention of his son and his "first" impressions of "Daddy" drove a spike into David's heart, making him resent the intrusion of his wife. There was too much guilt, too much anger, and far too much love beneath it all, to handle right now. He wanted nothing more than to be left alone with Matthew, so that he could be the master of whatever impression the child might have.

But he didn't want her to leave, either. He wanted her there at his side forever, never leaving, not even leaving his sight. She might never return if she left. They both might be gone. And now that he knew about his son and his wife was with him once more, a new separation might kill him.

Struggling to find something neutral to say, David laughed and asked, "Are kids' hands always sticky?"

"Yes," Nicole said, happy to join in his laughter. "I don't know how they do it, but they usually are."

For that moment, they were a family, guilt and re-crimination cast aside in the simple pleasure of their son's company.

GARTH DONNELLY maneuvered his chartered speed-boat south along the coast, hoping to catch up with the *Katharine* before she got too far away. The homing device secured in the bilge of the ship would allow him to track them over about a thirty-mile distance, but he wasn't in range yet, and so had to hurry to find them.

The kid would make sure there was some kind of light for him to track at night, too, but Garth didn't plan to continue this charade any longer than he had to. He would follow until they were safely beyond the U.S. Coast Guard patrol area, and then he would sink them. Now that they had the coordinates of the sat-ellite, the stubborn oceanographer and his family were nothing more than a loose end.

SUNSET REFLECTED brightly from Nicole's eyes as David regarded her over the table after dinner that evening. It lit her entire face with a soft glow that gave her the appearance of a porcelain figure, perfectly carved and smiling at him. The sight pained him, but it wasn't an uncomfortable pain at all. No, not at all.

Nicole couldn't read the expression in David's face. The setting sun had cast his face in shadows, leaving just a rose-colored outline of his noble jaw and a glimmer of light in his eyes. There was a mystery in that sight. What he was thinking was beyond knowing, but she knew what she hoped his thoughts might be.

She longed for him with even greater force than she had before. Throughout the day and the meal Jerry prepared for them, she had been beset by a growing desire that could only be restrained by the presence of two other men on ship with them. Two men, and one loud child.

Matthew was asleep now, however. She and David had put him to bed together, and she had marveled at how good he was with a child, even handling the diaper properly. He had kissed his son good-night and held Nicole to him as they watched Matt settle in on his seaborne bed.

The feeling of David's arm around her remained with her still. It was the first intimate touch they had shared since they had been reunited, and it had fanned the flames within her until she felt she might melt from the heat.

I missed him so terribly, she thought as Jerry cleared the dishes from the table. *Maybe we can leave it all as history and avoid fighting over the past. Maybe we can forgive each other and be a family.* It was clear that he loved his son. That had been her real worry about him, and it had obviously been groundless. *Maybe we can just be in love again.*

She did love him, and that was all she was worried about at the moment.

"We don't have anything suitable for dessert," Jerry told them when he returned from the galley. "Sorry about that."

"That's all right," Nicole said. "I try to avoid desserts."

"Why? You don't seem to have gained any weight," the man replied as he took his cup of coffee in hand.

"Not an ounce," David agreed.

"You guys are blind!" Nicole exclaimed. "My girlish figure is gone."

"Enhanced," David said, leaning back to switch on the cabin lights. He could see that her figure had changed, but not at all for the worse. She had indeed become more womanly with motherhood, and even more desirable in his loving eyes.

"No comment," Jerry put in. "I'm going to keep Ben company on the bridge. Are we still planning to go through the Canal?"

"Oh, yes, I'm not taking my son around the Cape in the winter."

"We'll keep on course then, Captain." He took the carafe of coffee and his cup to the hall door, then turned. "You know, we've got that bottle of brandy in the pantry," he said. "You might want to crack it open. Bye."

"Bye." David smiled, listening to the sound of his partner's retreat to the upper level of the boat. "Playing matchmaker, I guess," he said.

Nicole watched him, remembering the first time she'd seen that handsome face, when she was his lawyer's secretary and he was a mysterious stranger in from the sea. Her mysterious stranger had been restored to her, and she couldn't stop looking at his wonderful face.

"I'd like a little brandy," she said. "Just a bit."

"You'd better watch it, lady," David warned her. "You don't want to get tipsy, when you're shipboard with a sailor who hasn't been to port in a while."

"Really? And how long has it been since you were in port?" She watched him walk to the pantry and return with the bottle and two glasses. He moved like a great cat, rolling over the desk with muscular ease.

"About two years," he said, with no hint of bitterness in his voice. He removed the seal and worked the stopper from the bottle. Then he poured about a finger's depth into both of the glasses. "Two years," he repeated. "I only have one port."

"Yes, two years," she said, her own longing mirroring the feeling that shone in his eyes. She accepted the brandy and touched glasses with him.

"To shore leave," he said, an almost coy smile playing at the corners of his expressive lips. "And pulling into port."

"Shore leave," she replied.

They drank, and Nicole blinked a bit at the burn of liquor in her throat. The drink caused an immediate warmth in her stomach, building on the warmth in her heart.

"I missed you." He came around the table and took a seat beside her, his hand reaching instinctively to her shoulder and stroking down over her arm. "I'm glad that you're back home."

"David, I don't know what we can do to. . ."

"No, you don't need to know," he said, gripping her upper arm firmly. "I know what we can do. What we will do."

David pulled her to him, capturing her lips firmly with his and claiming them totally. He slipped his arm around her shoulders and grasped the back of her head with the other hand, holding her with a firmly possessive grip as their first kiss became another and another.

The restraint Nicole had possessed earlier evaporated in his arms, leaving the molten core of her desire exposed and willing before him. The hands that pulled her blouse from her jeans and slipped over the skin of her back were welcomed with a shudder and a sigh. And when he pulled her up to stand with him, pressing his body to hers, she rose with no more resistance than the air would have given to his movements. His hands were on her, his lips were nibbling at her throat, and she was lost in the sensation, her head thrown back in surrender.

David's passion grew with the feeling of her body against him, exciting him into abandoning all scruples and ideals of conduct. He pushed back from her slightly and tore her blouse open rather than pausing at the buttons and then slipped her bra up to cover her breasts with kisses instead.

"Oh, David," she whispered, clutching his head to her as his tongue created a circle of fire over one taut nipple. "Oh, not here," she managed to sigh, and then forgot the injunction as soon as the words left her mouth.

David had opened her jeans and slipped his hands down over her bottom, pulling her to him once more as he continued exciting her with lips and tongue. Then, with a convulsive movement, he lifted her up and folded her over his shoulder. He stalked back to his cabin, one hand holding the backs of her knees to his chest, while the other pulled at her denim trousers so that she was free of them by the time they'd reached sanctuary and he'd thrown her on the bed.

Once the cabin door closed behind them, it was as though they were transformed into pure emotion. Free of all constraints, they were nothing more than desire personified.

Nicole marveled at the feeling of her husband's body moving with a familiar silken friction within hers, the increasing tempo of his movement forcing her heart to step up its pace, as well. And her need of him grew in his tumultuous release within her, her desire growing hotter, and they rolled on the bed and she took charge of his body with a ferocity equal to his.

Theirs was no innocent teenage ideal of lovemaking, but the full-throated roar of adult love that only the intimacy of marriage can create. Theirs was a lovemaking that dared all things and knew no bounds beyond the shared sensation.

Hands cupped and caressed her swaying breasts as she moved back against him; lips teased his navel when she moved to the fore; bodies were united as though God had once made a mistake in creating their two separate bodies and God himself had commanded that they reunite as one.

Time was a foreign concept, and the bed seemed as immaterial as their bodies, for they were nothing more than two long-separated sparks destined to be united in a cataclysmic explosion that left them, at last, lying twined together, unspeaking, as the rocking motion of the ship lulled the lovers to sleep.

Above decks, beyond any knowing of the emotion that had been played out on the sailboat that night, Ben Tucker walked to the stern of the boat and switched on the aft running lights. He stood looking out to sea for a long moment, squinting toward the horizon, lit by a slim crescent of moon, as though searching for something following them in the night.

A brief flash in the darkness seemed to respond to his search, and then the young man returned to the wheelhouse to take Jerry's place at the helm.

Chapter Six

The air smelled of spices and fresh bread, and the tangy scent of pickles wafted through the air, amplified beyond normal importance. Something whirred, and she turned to see an older woman slicing meat behind the counter. The woman smiled at her, nodding, saying "Try the pastrami," with her voice stretching out the words like an old LP record being turned slowly by hand.

Looking down, Nicole saw that she was naked, and that her body was wet, and her hair was clinging damply to her head.

Something beyond her nakedness was wrong here, and Nicole kept turning, looking over the empty tables in the narrow deli, seeking something. Something. Matthew. He wasn't there, but he should be. She could hear him, but he wasn't in sight. She could hear him saying, "Daddy, daddy, daddy," over and over again.

And then David was standing against the wall, wearing a dark suit, eyes closed, hands folded over his stomach. Why didn't he open his eyes and answer his son?

She kept turning, not waiting for an answer, but turning around and around until the deli began to waver slightly around her. She was becoming dizzy from the movement, but couldn't seem to stop herself from turning until a man's hand on her chest stopped her cold and she found herself looking into the cold gray eyes of her blond assailant from the apartment house.

"Missing a young one, are you?" he asked, pressing her back so that she stumbled slightly. "Missing a wee nipper?" He touched her breast, smiling. "What will you do to get him back, honey?" Smiling, touching her.

"David!" she screamed. "David!"

In response to her call, David toppled forward and fell flat on the floor, like a man carved of wood.

"Wrong answer," the man said. "Wrong answer."

The walls blew outward, and she saw Matthew then. He was flying away from her, propelled by the force of the explosion, with an expression of fear and pain on his chubby face. "No!" she cried, reaching for her son. But he continued to fly away, growing smaller and smaller in the distance, framed by her outstretched hands.

"No!"

Waking seated in the bed, Nicole shivered and stared unseeing for a moment. "No..." she whispered.

"What's wrong?" David sat beside her, his hands immediately reaching to grasp her shoulders and hold her shivering form to him. "Bad dream?"

"Yes," she replied, dropping her head to nuzzle it against his hand on her shoulder. "I don't understand it. It was so strange."

"What was it about?"

"Well, I think I was in the deli in New York."

"Hoffman's?" he said, mentioning the establishment where their life together had begun.

"Yes, I think so. You were there, too, or maybe just a statue of you—I don't know—and that blond man, Donnelly, who was at my apartment. Then there was an explosion, and Matthew was flying away from me, and I couldn't reach him."

"That's a pretty involved dream," David commented, kissing her shoulder as he slipped his arms around her and held her close. "Anything else?"

"I was naked," she said. "And I was wet." Nicole laughed. "Of course, it makes no sense."

"Not yet," he said, "but you never know."

"Jerry said you dreamed about the earthquake," Nicole said. "What were those dreams like?"

"More just a feeling than anything concrete," he admitted. "I didn't actually dream about an earthquake, just that you were hurt. Actually, that you were dead," he said, in a faraway voice. "And I could never figure out why I heard a baby crying in the dream."

"I dreamed specifically about an earthquake," she said. "And I dreamed that some bearded man was calling to me from the ocean. He was trying to warn me. It turned out that the bearded man was you, and you were there to save me."

"And the baby in my dream was my own," he added.

"So this dream might..."

"Mean nothing," David said. "Or everything."

"Given our past history, I wouldn't discount the warning of the dream." She slipped her legs over the edge of the bed and stood. "I'd better check on Matthew."

Then she turned, perplexed. "I don't have a robe," she said. "Where are my pants and blouse?"

"I don't know." David leaned to look around the floor near the bed, seeing nothing. He sat looking at her, smiling. "You're naked," he said.

Nicole stopped, looking at herself, realizing that she had been turning around in circles looking for her clothing, just as she had been turning in her dream. And, just as in her dream, her son was not present, though she felt that he should be.

"I'm not wet," she said.

"But you're on a boat. There's plenty of water around us."

Nicole knelt hurriedly, finding her pants hidden by discarded bedding, her underwear caught within them. As she put them on hurriedly, she saw her blouse beside a chair, but it was torn—useless.

"Here." David grabbed a sweatshirt from his closet and tossed it to her as he struggled into his own clothing. They were both propelled by an urgency born of experience with dreams becoming reality, both anxious to avoid the worst of what might happen, while both hoped the fear was foolish.

And it was foolish, for Matthew was just stirring in his playpen when they entered the cabin, and he smiled up at them happily.

"There's the boy," David said, lifting his son. "There's my little tiger."

"I feel a bit silly now," Nicole admitted with relief. "But it seemed entirely possible that something was going to happen. Thank God we're wrong."

"We're not out of the woods yet, however," David cautioned her. "Morley Kraft has a long reach, and there's little we can do to stop him."

"Any man who would threaten the safety of a little child is a monster, no matter how long his reach or how many connections to power he has," Nicole stated as she took Matthew and began to change her son's diapers. "And the man who assaulted me was a heartless brute."

"Yes, Donnelly is a man we should stay well clear of."

"But we can't exactly do that, can we? God, David, you sound as though it will be easy to avoid them," Nicole snapped. "It's not. They're after us, and they aren't going to be stopped by a little distance."

"I know that," he said, tersely.

"If you know it, why make light of it?"

"I'm not making light of anything," he said. "The whole thing is a horrible mess, and the only way out of it is to dump you and Matt off someplace and go retrieve the satellite for Kraft."

"But you can't do that," she insisted. "It will only make certain he knows where to find you when your usefulness to him is finished. Haven't you thought this through at all?"

"Yes, I have, but I didn't realize there was a child involved until I found you. If I had known, I sure would have planned something different. You could have told me about Matt."

"Don't try to blame this on me, David!"

"I'm not. You've got nothing to do with Kraft, but you sure have something to do with me. Why didn't you tell me? Were you afraid I'd try to take him away from you?"

"Fat chance."

"I didn't say I wanted to take your son away," he said. "But you've given me pretty good legal grounds, by running off like a little fool, rather than just saying you were pregnant and giving me a decent chance to get used to the idea."

"I'm a fool now? No, you were very clear about your feelings about children, mister. You didn't want any. Period."

"A fair number of men would say they didn't want children at a given time in their lives, Nicole. It's not an unusual response. Dammit, how could you expect me to want kids running around on deck?"

"You've got a pretty big house in Connecticut for kids to run in, David. I don't see your problem."

"I meant aboard ship. I just needed to finish up the South Pacific survey before I could head back to land for any significant period of time. Don't you understand my point?"

"You didn't make that point before. No, you just said you didn't want kids. God, David, what was I supposed to do?"

"Oh, you're right," he said in a scoffing tone. "Running off to have the baby and raise it alone without telling me was the best plan you could have come up with. That's stupid."

"I wasn't going to hang around, hoping for a sympathetic reaction from you," she said. "That would have been stupid. If you didn't want kids, I wasn't going to impose them on you."

"Thank you for your kind consideration, dear," David said icily. "You've stolen most of my son's life from me, just because you didn't want to risk my reaction to your pregnancy."

"I already knew your reaction."

"No, you didn't. You knew my reaction to a hypothetical question. You had no idea what I might really want."

The two of them stood staring at each other for a moment, glaring into each other's eyes, with frustrated need heating the air between them. Then Matthew began to cry, and Nicole scooped him into her arms.

"Look what you've done now," she said. "He's not used to arguments."

"Well, I'm not used to being stabbed in the back by someone who says she loves me," David said. "I've got good reason to argue."

"Keep it up and you'll lose us again," Nicole said with soft anger as she stroked the back of her son's head. "But then, that's probably what you want, anyway."

"The two of you aren't going anywhere," he replied. "We'll either work this out or we won't, but you're not leaving me again." Then he turned and left the cabin.

Nicole stood with her son, wondering for a moment whether to take that last remark as a threat or a promise. Did it mark his love for them, or the conclusion of that love?

"Now, now, Matthew," she cooed to her son. "You're fine. Everything is all right."

But it was entirely possible that nothing would ever be *all right* again.

DAVID ASSUMED CONTROL of the wheel of the *Katharine* and stared stonily out to sea as they made their way along the coast toward Mexico. If he could find a safe place to put Nicole and Matthew off, he would be free to deal with Morley Kraft from a somewhat less vulnerable position. It would be best to put a bit of distance between him and his wife once more, anyway. At least until he was better able to control his anger over his son.

It wasn't fair. But then, life wasn't fair, and nobody had ever told him that it would be.

It was hard to be so angry with someone he loved so much. Even telling her he loved her was hard, with so much resentment boiling within him.

He had to get over the past—that was all there was to it—get over it and move on. The fact was that he loved Nicole more than ever, and could think of no other woman but her. And as for his son, well, his feeling about Matthew could most easily be described as a feeling of awe.

Get over it, Buster. Grow up and get over it.

David switched on the marine radio and tuned it to a weather frequency. The day was fair, and the sea calm, but he didn't trust them to remain that way. There was a child on board to be considered.

The announcer's words came over the air, faintly, static obscuring his words. David rolled the tuning knob back and forth, thinking the contact might be dirty, but couldn't improve the reception. It seemed that the static was rhythmic, too, more of a pulse than simple interference.

David's brow creased in worry. Why would he be picking up a rhythmic pulse of some kind?

He hit the intercom switch. "Jerry, come up to the bridge."

David locked the ship's autopilot on course and rummaged through a storage cabinet for a piece of equipment while he waited for the other oceanographer to come up. He found what he was looking for— a small plastic box with a tube like a microphone extending from one end, with a dial and a needle pointer on the face. When he switched it on, it made a small beep, and the needle began to twitch slightly.

"What's up?" Jerry came into the cabin and stood beside him, looking at the box in his hand. "What's the deal with the signal locator?"

"Just a hunch. Listen to the radio for a minute," David said as he slowly turned a knob on his instrument to change the frequency it was receiving. "Hear that static?"

"Yes. I suppose the antenna worked loose."

"No, I don't think so. Don't you hear how rhythmic the static is?"

"You know I've got no sense of rhythm."

"Seriously," David said. "Okay, I think I've got this tuned. Come on, let's see what's going on."

NICOLE SAT in her cabin with Matthew in her arms, watching the light clouds drift by through the small porthole. This wasn't what she wanted for her life. Not to be so close to perfection, yet apparently unable to attain it.

David Germaine was the only man she would ever love. She knew that as surely as she knew that she was breathing. Yet she couldn't seem to get over the rift that had come between them. Was she wrong about him? Or was his vision about his own feelings clouded by hindsight? She would never know, and would have to accept that and go on with her life if she wanted to have a life at all.

Matthew deserved a father, and she wanted her husband back. Maybe it was time to swallow her pride and accept the love he offered. It was clear, for one thing, that he did love his little son. There was no mistaking that in his eyes when he looked at the child.

Did he still love her, as well?

"Well, kiddo, it's about time for breakfast," she told Matt. It was clear from his squirming that he wasn't about to sit here doing nothing for much longer. "Let's go."

There were footsteps on the deck above her, some-one walking slowly and pausing often. Then they stopped.

"Let's see what they're up to." She stood and carried her son into the hall and up through the salon to the deck, taking him along the narrow passage between the upper cabin and the railing guarding her from a misstep that could plunge them into the sea.

"Here," David was saying to Jerry and Ben, who leaned over a box in his hand. "Right here."

"What's wrong?" Nicole asked.

The men turned to look at her and the child for a moment, and then David said, "What are you bringing him along here for? Nicole, you might go overboard."

"I do have some experience carrying a child," she countered. "What are you guys doing?"

"We think we've found a transmitter," Jerry told her.

"What?"

"Here. Look." David held the box in his hand out so that she could see it. The needle anchored to the center of the compasslike dial was pointing straight out from the boat and quivering slightly. "Now watch the needle."

He moved the box from side to side, and the needle moved to account for the movement so that it was always aimed at the same point of the horizon.

"Someone out there sending a signal?" she asked.

"No. Watch the needle," he said.

David leaned against the railing and extended the box out from the ship, tilting it slightly so that they could still see the dial on top. Instead of continuing to point out to sea, the needle swung sharply around to point right back at them!

"We're transmitting?"

"Yes, we are," David said ominously. "Jerry, change course. Take us in to San Diego at top speed. Ben, grab the long boat hook and bring it out here."

"Right on," the young man said, and hurried toward the stern.

David peered over the edge into the water moving along the side of the boat. "I can't see anything down there," he told her, "but it's got to be there. Unless it's in the bilge, of course, but nobody could have gotten on board to plant a homing transmitter there."

"So they're following us?"

"Yes," he said simply. "They're following us."

Ben hurried around with the long wooden pole with a steel point and hook at the end. He traded it for the receiving device David had been using and then stood back with a pensive frown on his face.

David held the ten-foot pole down and pressed it to scrape along the side of the boat beneath the waterline. Back and forth he went with the pole. Then he stopped a moment.

"I think I hit something that time," he said. He rubbed the pole roughly against the ship several times. "I think I..." He pressed down on the tool. "Yes, I think I got it. Ben? What's the receiver doing now?"

"Nothing. No, wait, it's turning," Ben said. "It seems to have lost the signal. It's just drifting now."

"I sank the beacon," David said. "Too much water over it now."

"But if we lost the signal, that means whoever is following us lost it, too," Nicole said. "They'll know we found it."

"Yes, and that's why we're headed toward shore as fast as we can run. Let's get inside."

When they threw open the door to the bridge, the radio announcer's voice greeted them. "Fair skies and winds of one or two knots throughout the afternoon," he was saying clearly. "Minor squalls possible into the night."

David switched off the radio. "We're about fifteen miles out to sea right now," he said. "But we can be docked in San Diego in less than an hour. Just let them try homing in on us on a jetliner."

"They may not have to, boss," Ben yelled from on deck. "There's a speedboat gaining astern."

"Damn!" David grabbed the binoculars and ran out onto the deck to look back along their wake. "It's Donnelly. Jerry, get on the horn to the Coast Guard. Send out a distress signal." He ran back into the cabin and began throwing cabinets open, searching for something. "Nicole, tie yourself and Matt into a couple of life vests and wait in the salon."

"What are you going to do?" She was frozen, her child pressed tightly to her bosom, as she watched him.

"I don't know. I've got a small rifle in the salon, but I can't remember where the bullets for it are. I may not have any."

"You can't shoot him!"

"I damn well can shoot him," David said forcefully. "But not without bullets." He stood, kicking the cabinet door shut angrily. "All I've got is a flare pistol. Go on, get ready," he commanded her.

Nicole complied, finding the life vests in the locker in the salon and tying the overlarge garment onto Matthew. Then she put her own vest on and watched out the large ports in the main cabin.

The speedboat was already drawing near them, the roar of its engine clear over the throbbing sound of the *Katharine*'s own engines. Garth Donnelly stood at the wheel, grinning as he came near.

Nicole was transfixed by the sight of that hated man coming so close to her son. Her blood was chilled by the sight of him and the memory of his threats.

"What do you want?" she heard David shouting from on deck. "I'm not giving you any information."

"Don't need it, mate!" Donnelly's voice was harsh with triumph. "I just happened to notice my transmitter go dead and figured that you found it."

Nicole leaned to watch out the window. Donnelly's boat was about five feet away from them, the man himself standing cockily at the helm, steering with one hand to maintain his position alongside the moving ship.

"Hi, Benny," the blond man shouted. "I've got your pay."

"You're supposed to leave everyone alone," the student shouted back. "That was the deal."

"Yes, and Morley Kraft never breaks a deal. But you never had a deal with me, did you?" He laughed, throwing his head back in evil mirth. "Goodbye, all."

The man let go of the wheel, allowing his boat to slow and drift back along the ship while he picked up a satchel from his feet. Ben ran along the deck, past the salon port, keeping abreast of the speedboat, with David following him. As he passed, Nicole could see that David was holding the flare pistol in one hand, slightly behind him, his finger tense on the trigger. Then her attention was captured by a sudden movement on the speedboat.

Garth Donnelly tugged at a string extending from within the satchel and then lobbed it up onto the rear deck of the *Katharine* where it bounced back beneath the large wooden wheel at the stern.

"No!" Ben began to run toward it, but Garth was ready for that, too. He raised a black machine pistol and fired, the nasty *brak-ak-ak-ak* of the weapon biting through the air.

The bullets knocked Ben to one side, and he slipped to the deck and grasped the satchel before him. Then he stood uncertainly, his eyes unfocused as he clutched the satchel and tried to stagger to the rail with it. Garth fired again, and Ben fell to the deck.

David dived through the salon door toward Nicole and Matthew. "Down!" he screamed, seconds before the blast.

Glass showered over them in the deafening roar of the explosion, and Nicole waited a second, hunched over her son, until it seemed that the worst had passed. Then she opened her eyes.

Fire engulfed the rear of the ship, and David lay just within the cabin, slowly lifting himself up and shaking his head groggily. His flare pistol lay on the floor beside him.

Suddenly, Nicole was filled with a rage such as she'd never experienced before. She sat Matthew on the deck and grabbed the pistol and ran with it to the cabin and out toward the fire.

Donnelly's speedboat was pulling away, headed toward Mexico. She had only seconds, and leveled the weapon toward him with her arm extended, just as her father had taught her to shoot years ago. Then she lifted it slightly, allowing for the heavy projectile it would fire, and pulled the trigger.

The pistol made a loud popping sound, and the flare sped out, trailing a plume of gray smoke. A second later, Nicole was rewarded by a flash of light in the rear of the speedboat, and then the brighter light of flames as Donnelly's boat, too, began to burn.

"Good shooting!" Jerry called out to her from the cabin. "Come on! We've got to abandon ship before the fire hits the fuel! You take Matt, while I get David moving."

David was sitting on the floor blinking and shaking his head. The back of his shirt was peppered with pink spots where glass had struck him, and a cut bled freely behind his left ear.

"Inflate the raft, Jerry," he said. "I'll be with you in a minute."

"Come on now!" Nicole insisted, picking Matthew up.

"You go with Jerry and deploy the raft. I'll be there!"

He stood then, looking stronger. And then he pushed her along toward the bridge where the scientist was already making ready for their escape. "Get out of here!" he shouted, and she obeyed without further protest.

Jerry had inflated the raft and was holding it against the side of the ship when Nicole came out of the bridge.

The *Katharine* was listing heavily to the stern, where the blast had torn a gash in the hull, below the waterline. For a moment, Nicole harbored the faint hope that the water would put out the fire, but that hope was dashed when the fuel leaking from the tanks burst into flames with a soft *whump!*

"Come on!" Jerry dropped the raft into the water, holding the line, and then tugged at her arm to get her to climb into it. "Before the fuel drifts around us."

Nicole climbed carefully over the rail with her son and held on a moment. Then she dropped about six feet into the large yellow rubber raft below them. She was calmed somewhat to see that it was equipped with a small outboard motor that would help their escape.

"What about David?" she cried as Jerry jumped in and switched on the battery-powered motor. "Wait for David!"

"We'll wait at a safe distance," he said. "He can swim, Nicole."

They moved slowly away from the stricken ship as the burning fuel floating atop the sea began to encircle it. On board, about fifteen feet to the rear now, David burst through the door to the bridge with a dark plastic bag in his hand.

"The baby book!" Nicole cried out in surprise and alarm. "He went for the baby book!"

"Here!" David shouted. He swung the bag around twice in a circle beside him and then let go, sending it sailing in a high arc toward the raft. Jerry stood uncertainly, diving nearly overboard and catching the bag before it hit the water. He dropped it into the bottom of the raft and grabbed the tiller again.

They were nearly thirty feet away now, and moving fast as David prepared to jump overboard. The flames had circled the ship entirely as he stood with one foot up on the rail of the vessel, which was tilting away from them, barnacles on the hull visible above the water. Flames of about three feet rose around him, and he paused a moment taking several deep breaths. Then he looked over his shoulder at the ship, which shook beneath his feet.

"David!" Nicole screamed out as she saw him dive into the flaming water.

A second after he disappeared beneath the water, the *Katharine*'s fuel tanks exploded, a flaming geyser of water shooting fifty feet into the air as the wooden vessel splintered and rolled over in the sea.

A moment later, the ship was gone. Nothing but a patch of flaming debris marked the spot where it had been.

Chapter Seven

Nicole stared anxiously at the flames dancing on the water where the ship had been floating moments before. The sound of the blast still rang in her ears, and Matthew was looking around them, eagerly searching for the source of the sound that had made him start in her arms.

Even he was quiet in the aftermath of the blast, and the two adults searched the water for some sign that David was all right.

Just as Nicole was beginning to fear the worst, her husband burst through the surface of the water about five feet away from the raft, with a great whooshing intake of air.

"Whoa!" David called out as he swam three halting strokes to the raft and grasped the nylon rope threaded through grommets along the top of the inflated sides. "Oh, hell," he gasped, hanging on with both arms hooked limply over the raft. "I've got to get more exercise."

"Get in," Jerry said.

"Wait." David hung there, breathing heavily with his face pressed against the side of the raft. "I haven't got the strength to get in. Not yet."

"You risked your life for the baby book?" Nicole asked him. "Are you crazy?"

"Hey, it's my kid's life," he said weakly, lifting his head to smile up at her. "You've got video," he said. "You didn't tell me you had video."

"It didn't come up. Are we going to argue about that now?"

"No, just mentioning it, is all. Okay," he said, gripping the side of the raft tighter. "I'll give it a try. You guys scrunch over to the other side of the raft, so I don't flip us."

They moved over, and David pulled himself up to his belly on the raft and then rolled over to lie panting inside, water running from his clothing to form a pool in the raft.

"You know, at least before you got in we were dry," Jerry commented.

"My heart bleeds for you," David laughed. "You were dry, and now you're wet."

"We're wet," Nicole said quietly as the water puddled around her and soaked through her jeans. "We've had an explosion and gotten wet. Garth Donnelly was there, and you were lying facedown on the floor." She looked at David, nodding. "It's the dream."

"But Matt is right here."

"I know," she admitted, "but somehow that doesn't comfort me very much right now."

She knew that she shouldn't be worried. They had survived intact, while it didn't seem possible that Garth Donnelly could have survived the fate of his boat. The last they'd seen of him was his flaming speedboat rushing in the direction of Mexico. Still, they hadn't seen it sink. Hadn't actually seen what happened to the evil man.

Until she knew his fate, there could be no comfort.

SATURDAY MORNING provided Matthew with the biggest thrill of his young life. Dressed in brand-new clothing, he boarded a flight from San Diego to New York City with his parents and Jerry. He squirmed and jumped in Nicole's lap to look around at the other passengers while they waited to take off.

Then the jet engines began to work, building to a rumbling roar that shivered through the plane as they began moving slowly into position to take off. Seated at the window with his mother, the young traveler stared around the cabin at first, his mouth open in wonder. Then Nicole directed his attention out the window, and he saw the ground moving beyond the plane's massive wing.

When the ground began to drop away beneath them, and the actual feeling of movement was gone, Matt shouted out happily and pointed at the miracle outside the window. Even more miraculous, however, were the plastic-wrapped crackers that were brought to him, along with half a glass of juice to drink, and he was soon absorbed in the task of unwrapping and consuming his treat.

Nicole sat back, watching Matthew maneuver the crackers out of the wrapping, once she'd split the seam for him. She could see out of the corner of her eye that David was watching him, too, a small smile playing at his lips.

Seated across the aisle from them, Jerry Brunsvold had tilted his seat back a bit and was attempting to get to sleep, and all the other passengers were settling in for the flight.

"Do you think we're safe now?" Nicole asked David after a moment. "They apparently got the position of the satellite from Ben, so they don't need you to get it any longer."

"We might be safe, I suppose," David mused. "If Donnelly is dead, Kraft can just disavow anything we might claim against him."

"*If* he's dead?"

"They found the wreckage, but they don't have a body yet," David said grimly.

The Coast Guard had, indeed, found the burned hulk of Donnelly's speedboat drifting about a mile out to sea, along the Mexican coast. As soon as the Coast Guard cutter picked them up, they had dispatched their own speedboat in pursuit of the man, and had found the wreck within the hour. But there had been no sign of Donnelly.

They had spent the remainder of the day answering questions about the fire and explosion and filling out insurance forms and having money wired to them from the East Coast so that they could get hotel rooms and clothing and the airline tickets that were taking them east now.

It had been at the police station in San Diego that they learned of the assault on Paul Gabriel. The student was in guarded condition in a San Francisco hospital, and David had made arrangements for his parents to join him there.

The authorities had taken their statements and listed Donnelly as being wanted for questioning about both attacks, but it was assumed that he was dead, so they weren't planning any active search.

"If he is dead, Kraft has no reason to bother us again, does he?" Nicole was hoping against hope for a positive answer, though she feared that there would be none.

"Well, we would never be able to prove that he ordered Donnelly to kill Ben or attack Paul. He probably didn't, for that matter. And now that they've sunk my ship, all the gear for retrieving the satellite is gone, so I can't help them."

"You look worried, though. What's wrong?"

"I wonder about the coordinates he has for the satellite. Ben wasn't with us last summer, when we found it, and he wasn't around when I first contacted the Department of Defense about the location. I can't think of how he might possibly have known where it is."

"Snooping around, I imagine."

"No, I don't have them written down anywhere. I sent the only notes I had to the government." He tapped his temple with his index finger. "They're just in my head now," he said.

"You don't suppose Ben lied to Kraft?"

"I think he must have."

"Oh, that's sad," Nicole said. "I thought he double-crossed you, but it may be that he was trying to get them off your back."

"Or he was playing both ends against the middle," David said. "I would assume that Kraft paid a nice wad of cash for the information. When it was proved wrong, Ben could always have claimed that I tricked him."

"The boy is dead," she said. "I'd prefer to think the best of him now."

"So would I, but we can't afford to cloud our judgment at the moment. When Kraft finds out he's got the wrong location, he'll be ready to blame someone. And he'll be even more anxious to get the proper coordinates. It'll be harder for him to maneuver, now that Donnelly's activities have shed some light on things, but he's still not personally connected. I can't prove a thing against him."

"Gee, don't try to make me feel any better or anything," Nicole said, stroking Matt's hair as the boy finished his crackers. "I was just starting to feel relaxed."

"Go ahead and relax," David said. "Nothing will happen to us up here. It's when we land that we're going to have to be careful."

Matt yawned and lay back against Nicole to smile up at David. He patted David's arm, yawning again, and fell asleep, still reaching out to touch his father.

David smiled. "Take your cue from Matt and Jerry, and rest a bit. You've had an exciting couple of days."

"We all have," she said. She did, indeed, feel tired. A bone-deep fatigue seemed to settle in once Matthew began to slumber against her. It would be nice to sleep a bit.

David tried to rest, but couldn't do it. When they landed, he would put a call through to Morley Kraft and discuss the matter. His office at home was equipped with a telephone recording device he used to keep notes on teleconferences, and he might be able to obtain something incriminating that way. Either way, he had to find a way to end this nightmare once and for all.

MORLEY KRAFT was a balding man in his late fifties with an athletic build and a competitor's way of looking at the world. To his way of thinking, there were winners and there were losers in life, and he had always counted himself among the winners. He wasn't about to change that opinion now.

It was getting close, however.

His problems had begun with wool.

Australia had held the position as the world's preeminent supplier of wool for over a century, and would probably never lose that distinction. Wool was far and away the island continent's primary export. But, while wool remained a staple for fine garments, the market for wool was susceptible to the same ebb and flow as any market. When the world economy slipped, the use of wool slipped with it, as the material was replaced by cheaper synthetics.

This was a catastrophe for Australia, but even more so for Morley Kraft. He had been hiding a major portion of his income in the wool futures market by buying and selling shares with himself through a series of dummy corporations. When the market fell, he hadn't just fallen once. No, he'd fallen several times over, as each of his many deals lost value and his losses were compounded. By the time he was able to extract himself from the market, his fortune had been cut to a quarter.

And the sudden lack of funds had caused his other ventures to lose value, and soon, like a house of cards, his entire worldwide organization had been tottering and ready to fall. It seemed that the only thing that could still turn a profit these days was the sale of high-tech weapon systems, and even his company in that line was in danger of falling into the same black hole as the rest of his empire.

But then he'd heard from one of his contacts in the U.S. government about a multibillion-dollar satellite whose launch from Vandenberg Air Force Base had been aborted over the Pacific. The satellite, which should have been destroyed when the rocket was blown up, had turned up nearly intact. Best of all, the Department of Defense wasn't interested in salvaging it.

Morley Kraft, however, was more than willing to bring the satellite up from the bottom of the ocean. All he needed to know was its location.

Finding out that information had seemed like an easy task, but it was fast becoming the one thing that might break him. And if he didn't find out quickly, there would be no time to make use of the satellite if he did retrieve it.

He glanced at the newspaper in his hand one more time, then cast it aside. He stood and walked around

The Dreamer's Kiss   107

his desk to stare out the window at the rain that had been lashing at Sydney all morning. The weather was beastly, and he didn't expect that salvage operations in the South Pacific would be any too easy at this time. If that foolish scientist had just helped him to begin with, it would have been easy, but they were into the storm season now. The stubborn oceanographer had created a critical delay.

And now the young ship's mate had delayed him again by providing the wrong coordinates for the crash site. The survey ship he'd sent had found nothing. If the boy had thought he was pulling a fast one on Morley Kraft, he had been sadly mistaken. And if he had thought he could spare his friends even a second of the punishment they deserved for delaying Morley's plans, he'd been a fool.

But he was a dead fool by now, wasn't he?

Morley Kraft smiled. Although Donnelly had messed up his assignment, it had all turned out for the best. The boy, Ben, was dead, and the scientist was still alive. And, while the survivors had probably wasted no time in blaming him for their troubles, they still had no proof. All their claims were against Garth Donnelly and, as far as anyone knew, Donnelly was as dead as the oceanographer's shipmate.

Morley hadn't heard anything from Donnelly and, just like the authorities, assumed him dead. While he would miss his able assistance, it was certainly better that the man be dead than that he be alive and able to bear witness against his employer.

The telephone rang, and Kraft turned abruptly away from the window to answer it.

"Yes," he said harshly. He listened for a moment, a smile flickering at his lips and then slipping away. "Yes, by all means, do meet their flight. I trust you will be able to complete your task properly. Yes, certainly," he responded once more. "I shall be awaiting your call."

He hung up the telephone and pursed his lips in thought. Soon he would have the leverage he needed to force the oceanographer's hand. He nearly smiled, but the headline of the discarded newspaper lying on his desk stopped him.

Kraft Enterprises Investigated For Fraud, it read.

Between the investigation and the buyers impatiently awaiting delivery of the program he'd promised, Morley might almost have become nervous. But nervousness was something for losers, and Morley Kraft wasn't ready to consign himself to that heap just yet. No, he had a couple of aces to play yet. In half an hour's time, his operatives in New York would play his hand. Woe be it for anyone who thought he was bluffing.

MATTHEW WAS FLYING away from her, his screams filling her ears as she struggled to run after him through the tangle of rectangular objects strewn in her path. She couldn't run fast enough or reach far enough to get him, and suddenly he was gone, and she was standing in total silence, while the world around her evaporated into a black void. She was lost in a vacuum of despair, so lost that she couldn't move and wouldn't know what direction to go in if she could move.

And, as she stood immobile, she began to dissolve, as well. As though she had no purpose without her son, her body was melting away, so that soon there would be nothing to mark her passage through the world but the memory of her existence. Perhaps that would melt, too. Perhaps she had never really existed at all.

Maybe she had died on September 6, three years ago, after all, and everything since then had just been some hellish torture, to pay for some forgotten sin.

All she knew was that her son was gone.

"Hey! Mama!" A tiny fist struck her cheek, and Nicole started away to regard her son's laughing face. "Mama, Mama."

"Oh, boy, you're here, aren't you?" She hugged Matt, kissing his forehead, and then blinked herself more fully awake. "When do we land?" she asked David, who was looking at the airline magazine.

"Twenty minutes or so," he said. "You guys slept well."

"Didn't you sleep?"

"No, I never could sleep on airplanes. Jerry nods off as soon as he gets within ten miles of the runway," he said, indicating the other man, still pleasantly slumbering across the aisle. "I've never been good at it."

Nicole accepted the explanation, though she rather suspected that worry had kept him awake, more than anything else. None of them had slept much the night before, so he was likely to be just as tired as she had been.

"I didn't snore or anything, did I?"

"No, dear, you didn't snore." He laughed. "Maybe that's why I can't sleep on planes. I'm afraid I'll embarrass myself by rattling the windows."

"I think that if anyone is capable of rattling the windows on an airplane, then it's time to find a different airline."

This isn't so hard, she thought. *It is possible for us to have a civil conversation and not waste time with recriminations.* But there was always the underlying fear that one of them would say something that would trigger the storm of guilt and anger that brewed between them. Until that problem was properly dealt with, there was no way that any conversation could ever be *normal.*

Matthew was looking out the window again, staring at New York City, moving beneath them now as the plane made its final approach to JFK. He didn't know that moments from now they would all be absorbed by that concrete maze, or that a great deal of his future life would be ruled by it. All he knew was that something interesting was happening beyond his window, and he didn't want to miss the show.

"I wonder what he thinks of all this?" David said. "Do kids this age know what's happening at all, or does he just think this is like television?"

"I don't know," she said. "It would be fun to be able to see things like a child does for just a day, wouldn't it? Everything would be so new and marvelous.''

"Everything would be on a fresh slate," he said. "And every day would be a new chance to start again. I'd like that."

"I would, too."

And the airplane carrying the newly united family swept down out of the sky, to bring them to earth nearly three thousand miles from the troubles they'd left behind them. But three thousand miles wasn't nearly enough distance.

NICOLE'S DREAMS haunted her as they disembarked the airplane for the crowded terminal. Every stranger seemed a potentially menacing presence, each glance a threatening appraisal. She looked around nervously, waiting for an attack that didn't come, as they moved through the crowd toward the entrance.

David was tense at her side, as well, and she could see that her nervousness was clearly echoed in her husband's demeanor. Only Jerry was acting as though there were anything normal about their situation. In fact, he was relieved that their lack of luggage allowed them to move directly to a cab without the hassle of the baggage-claim area.

Matthew, of course, had loved every minute of the trip so far. The crowds excited him, and he twisted and turned in Nicole's arms in an effort to see as much as possible.

They were halfway through the vast terminal when a vague feeling of foreboding overcame Nicole. More than her initial nervousness, this was a definite feeling of something menacing approaching. She glanced around them quickly, trying not to look as though she suspected anything, but she saw nothing.

It's just your nerves. You'll be all right in the cab.

But as soon as she had somewhat reassured herself, they struck.

A woman in a dark coat was suddenly in her path, smiling and holding her arms out wide. "Nicole!" she exclaimed with excessive familiarity, though Nicole had no recollection of ever seeing this woman before in her life. "How was your flight?"

Just as she came to them, touching Nicole's shoulder and leaning in to chuck Matt under the chin, there was another movement behind them and to the side. Something struck Nicole in the back of her left knee, buckling it, and the woman grabbed Matt firmly as she stumbled.

"No!" she cried out. But the person behind her pushed her forward, knocking her sprawling as her son was deftly twisted from her grasp.

She heard David shout above her, and she scrambled to her feet in time to see three men pushing him back as the woman moved quickly to lose herself in the crowd. Only Jerry was free to move, and he was hurrying in pursuit of the woman who had her child.

The three men who had blocked David dispersed as if on cue, moving off in three different directions so that soon they, too, had effectively disappeared into the crowd of travelers. Nicole took no further notice of them, however, for she was hurrying after her child.

The woman had moved through a throng of people rushing toward the departing flights, so Nicole's movement was hampered by having to walk directly into the path of the flow of people. She caught a glimpse of the woman once more as she passed through the entrance to the terminal, and hurried after her.

Outside, the brightness of the sunshine disoriented her for a moment, and she didn't know where to turn. She couldn't see the woman or Jerry anywhere.

"Where are they?" David was at her side then, fear tightening his voice as he looked frantically around. "I didn't see them at all, but I followed you out."

"I don't know, David, I— Oh, there!"

Nicole pointed and then began to run toward a woman in a dark coat, a child's blond head visible above her shoulder. The woman seemed not to be hurrying, but just waiting for a cab to pull up to the stand. That didn't seem right, but then, the best way to disguise her flight would be to stop running.

"My baby!" Nicole cried as she reached the woman and grasped her shoulder. "What do you think—"

But the woman turned in surprise, a look of alarm on her face as she clutched the child in her arms more tightly. And the child that met Nicole's anxious stare was not Matthew, but a little girl!

"What on earth do you want?" the woman asked. "Get back, lady, or I'll call the cops!"

"Sorry, I thought you were someone else," Nicole explained.

"Yeah, I'll bet you did. I don't want any strangers touching my kid."

Nicole backed off, accepting the comfort of David's arm around her shoulder as they both tried vainly to find the woman who had stolen their son. When Jerry Brunsvold came walking dejectedly toward them through the crowd, their last hope was dashed.

Matthew had been kidnapped.

Chapter Eight

"Go with Jerry," David told Nicole urgently.

"David, they've stolen our son!" she shouted, grabbing his arm frantically. She couldn't think of anything beyond that fact as she stood in the sunshine of a spring afternoon and clung to her husband. "What are we going to do?"

"I'm going to follow the woman with the kid," he said. He had made a point of turning his back on the woman and facing Nicole. "You go with Jerry, so they can contact you."

"What? Don't be stupid. That's not Matt!"

"No, but it's awfully coincidental that she is standing out here dressed the same as the kidnapper and holding a blond child, just waiting for her kid to be mistaken for Matthew. Is she still waiting for a cab?"

"Yes, but I don't see your point."

"A taxi pulled up right in front of her just after she spoke to you, Nicole, but she didn't get into it. Tell me what she's doing now."

"Waiting, that's all. David, are you sure?"

"No, but it makes sense. There's plenty of taxis around. She's waiting for someone else. When she does leave, I'm going to see where they go. Take this," he said, giving her the briefcase they'd purchased in San Diego to carry Matt's baby book and videotape. "Now you and Jerry get to the apartment and wait."

"I'll call the police," Jerry offered. "We should arrange for a trace on any calls."

"No," Nicole said. "We don't want to do anything like that."

"Yes, you should," David said. His voice became calmer as he spoke, his determination giving him a clarity of purpose that overcame his fears for his son. "They aren't going to harm Matthew."

"But if we call the police . . ."

"Morley Kraft is a cocky guy. He'll figure us to run scared when it comes to Matt. Call the cops, and wait at the apartment."

"How will we know what you're doing?"

"I'll call when I can."

Behind David, Nicole saw the woman with the child start walking toward the curb and out behind a cab that had just pulled up.

"She's leaving," Nicole told David. "It looks as if she's getting into a white sedan."

"Okay, I'm off." And he turned and ran, leaping into another cab pulling up to the curb before Nicole could say anything in reply. A moment later, both the white sedan and David's cab were gone, leaving Nicole standing with nothing but her son's baby book and a videotape of his first steps to console her.

NICOLE STOOD at the window of David's Manhattan apartment, looking out over the city, toward Central Park. Where in this great, vast city were her husband and son? Where could they possibly be? It seemed hopeless now, looking out over all that concrete and steel, the idea that David could find Matthew, the idea that anyone could help them at all.

Buck up, Nicole, you're not done yet.

David was right—they couldn't harm Matthew if they wanted David's cooperation. But they had no motive to return Matt until David was finished helping him. And once David retrieved the satellite, Kraft would have no motive to leave any of them alive. In fact, his attack on Paul Gabriel and the murder of Ben Tucker on the ship showed quite clearly how they dealt with loose ends.

She felt that they had done the right thing by calling the police. Though she had been worried about the police being seen coming to the apartment, the arrival of two officers in jeans and casual shirts had put her greatly at ease. The two men had even arrived separately.

Once they were inside, however, their attitude had been anything but casual. They had obtained their information with brisk efficiency, while still maintaining a human tone, and had managed to instill a flicker of hope in Nicole's heart by the time they left again.

They had set up a trace on the telephone line so that they would know instantly where any incoming call originated, and then left to begin the work of finding her son.

Now, however, two hours after the departure of the policemen, Nicole had lost hope again, and she cast a bleak eye on the city beyond the window. There were too many people and too many square miles of concrete to search, and it was entirely possible that Matthew wasn't even in the city any longer.

For his part, Jerry sat in a ladder-back chair near the telephone, staring at the instrument as though willing it to ring. He would get up, pace a bit, come to pat Nicole's shoulder and offer a glum word of support, but he would always return to his chair and his vigil at the phone.

But no matter how much they wanted it to ring, the telephone remained silent.

"You'd think David would at least call," Nicole said. She found that she, too, had taken a position near the phone and was staring at it. "It's been over three hours."

"I think the lack of a call from David suggests that there is still hope that he's making progress," Jerry offered. "If he's still following her, he probably didn't have time to call. If, however, he lost her, or she proved to be a dead end, then he would have had plenty of time to call us."

"I suppose you're right, but that doesn't help the waiting, does it?"

"No," he agreed, "it doesn't help at all."

At 3:20 they were jolted away from their vigil at the phone by the buzzing of the intercom from the downstairs entrance.

"Yes?" Nicole was at the speaker box mounted near the door in a flash.

"Delivery," a man said.

"Bring it up." She pressed the release for the door and turned to look at Jerry, who shrugged in reply to the silent query in her eyes.

Minutes later, there was a knock at the door, and Nicole opened it to a youth in a windbreaker carrying a package wrapped in brown paper. It appeared to be a flat box about the size a department store might pack a shirt in. "Here you go," he said. "Sign here, please."

"Did you see who left this package?" Nicole signed his form, and Jerry reached past her to hand the fellow a tip.

"No, I . . . Well, I guess I did," he said. "He was a short guy in a dark overcoat. Kinda overdressed for the weather."

"Anything unusual about him?"

"Not that I can think of. You could call the office. Somebody might know." He shrugged, pocketing his tip. "We get a lot of deliveries."

"Yes, I'm sure. Thank you," Nicole said, closing the door and turning to Jerry with the package.

"Don't open it yet," he cautioned.

"Why not?"

"Let me check it first." He took the box from her, hefting it studiously. "Not much weight," he said as he walked through to the living room and placed it on the coffee table. Then he hurried out of the room, returning a minute later with an instrument much like the radio locator David had used on the ship.

"What are you doing?"

"A quick check for metal," he said. "I know it doesn't mean much, since you don't actually need metal to make a bomb, but I'd rather be safe."

"A bomb?"

"Don't act so surprised," Jerry said. "Maybe he does have the true coordinates for the satellite, and the kidnapping is just part of a plan to split us up and get rid of us."

"No, if David didn't have any written record of the site and never told Ben, I don't think Morley Kraft could possibly have the right location. He needs us," Nicole said, forcing herself to speak with greater conviction than she felt. If Jerry's possibility was correct, and the Australian millionaire's plan was merely to kill them, that would mean that Matt was probably... No, she couldn't even contemplate that possibility.

Jerry scanned the package, getting no response from the instrument in his hand. When he was finally satisfied that the package did not contain any kind of metal parts, he put the instrument aside and looked at Nicole.

"Well, I don't have any of the stuff I'd need to sniff for explosives," he said. "I guess all we can do is open the damn thing."

Nicole moved to tear at the paper taped over the box, but he stopped her. "Allow me," he said. "In fact, I'd feel better if you'd stand in back of me."

"Don't be so paranoid," she told him. His concern for her was touching, however, and she smiled at his gallantry.

Jerry tore the paper open and lifted a rather rumpled copy of the *Wall Street Journal,* dated two days earlier.

"What is that?" she asked.

"I guess they want us to catch up on old news."

Nicole removed the paper and, sweeping the box and wrapping onto the floor, unfolded the newspaper and began reading it over.

"It looks like he pulled this out of somebody's trash," Nicole said. "I suppose that would make it even harder to trace the origin."

"They don't miss a trick," the scientist said. Then his glance jumped down the page, and he cried out, "There! This is the ransom note!"

Nicole looked at the spot where he was pointing, in the lower part of the page. The word *central* was circled in blue pencil within one of the sentences of a report on banking regulations.

"Get a pen," she said, looking over the page once more. "We'll have to put their note together."

No other words were circled on the first page, but *park* was circled on page two.

"Central Park," she said, looking over page three and then turning to four. "Here, they've circled *nine* on page five."

Jerry wrote the words down as she found them.

"That's it," Nicole said as she flipped the final page of the paper shut.

"Central Park," Jerry read back from his sheet. "Nine p.m. One million used, out-of-sequence bills. No police."

"Well, that's pretty straightforward, isn't it?"

"Yes, but I don't know how they think we'll get the money this late in the day."

"They don't want the money," she said. "This is just a smoke screen to cover the real reason for the kidnapping."

"What do you mean?"

"We told the police that Morley Kraft wants to use my son as leverage against David to obtain the location of the satellite, right? Well, now someone comes along asking for ransom, and that makes our explanation look totally out of whack."

"You have a point," he said. "Especially given the fact of David's recent history of unsubstantiated complaints about Kraft pressuring him with threats. The police will be looking in the entirely wrong direction if we tell them about this message."

"We have to tell them," Nicole insisted.

"But it's a red herring."

"What if it's not? What if the kidnapping really is unrelated to Kraft and the satellite?"

"That's unlikely," Jerry said, shaking his head. "A coincidence of this magnitude is entirely improbable."

"But not impossible. No, I think we should tell the police and let the chips fall where they may. My most important task now is to get Matthew back. I'll worry about Kraft later."

"Right." He picked up the telephone and began dialing the number the detectives had left for them. "I'll fill them in and then get to work finding some cash."

"A million dollars? Can you come up with that so fast?"

"I don't know, actually," he admitted as he waited for his call to be answered. "But I'll sure give it the old college try."

Nicole returned to the window and her pensive watch over the city. It was a quarter to four now. Time was running short, if they hoped to have the money together for a 9:00 p.m. rendezvous with the kidnappers. Would they hear from David before then, so that he would know what had happened since he'd taken off in pursuit of the woman at the airport?

Where was David right now?

Jerry had gotten off the phone after making several calls, and he came to her side now. "I've got money on the way," he assured her. "Our insurance carrier is going to work with us on this. The *Katharine* was covered against acts of sabotage and piracy, so we've got that claim coming. And David still has a clause in his policy regarding kidnapping from when he was a child."

"Kidnapping? Why?"

"You've apparently forgotten his family." Jerry laughed. "There's a long line of robber barons in his family tree, and they got nervous about such things. Especially after the Lindbergh case. Everyone in the family was insured against kidnapping."

"But Matt isn't covered, is he?"

"No, not specifically, but he's David's son. Our agent is willing to come up with the cash now and take up the fine points of the policy with his bosses tomorrow."

"That's awfully good service," she said.

"You get what you pay for," Jerry said with another laugh. "Besides, they know they'll have to pay out on the *Katharine*. If we pay the ransom and the company decides that the coverage doesn't extend to Matt, they'll just take it out of the boat payment."

"At least we'll be able to bring something to the park tonight," Nicole said. "But I'd feel better if David were here."

But he wasn't, and there was no sign that he would be at her side any time soon. She missed him now more horribly than she ever had while parted from him, and that, coupled with the cruel kidnapping of her son, made the pain in her heart nearly too much to bear.

She had only just begun to think that there was a possibility for her little family to become one, and now this had to happen. Morley Kraft had better hope that the authorities punish him severely, for if they didn't he would have to deal with her anger. The way she felt right now, she couldn't think of a single human being she hated more than the Australian millionaire whom she'd never met.

And she didn't know of anyone who deserved the punishment of hell more than he did.

Chapter Nine

David Germaine got into the back of a cab that pulled up to the curb just as he got there and held a hundred-dollar bill across the seat to the driver.

"Follow that white Ford," he said, pointing. "If you don't lose them and don't get spotted, I'll give you another hundred."

"I still gotta run the meter...."

"Run the meter, too, just follow that car."

He sat hunched forward nervously as the Ford sedan left the terminal building and joined the traffic on the way out of the parking area. They weren't driving as though they suspected a tail, and he hoped that was a good sign. Either it meant that they didn't expect anyone to see through their act with the child, or it meant that he was wrong and the woman really did have nothing to do with his son's kidnapping.

But it was too coincidental for her to be there, dressed just as the kidnapper had been, and holding a child that looked so like his son from a distance. She had, after all, kept the child concealed, so that only the top of her blond head was in view to anyone coming out of the terminal.

More telling than that, however, was that the woman had made no move to distance herself from Nicole, as any mother would if she perceived a threat to her child. No, this woman had stood and played her act through to the end, without even clutching the girl more closely to her.

Still, he could be wrong. If he was, he was wasting more time than he could afford to waste, chasing a dead end.

David counted his money as unobtrusively as possible to be certain he had the cash to cover his sudden trip. He couldn't remember how much of the money they'd had wired to them in San Diego he had given to Nicole and Jerry. Since he had been carrying his wallet when he dived from the boat, he had his plastic, but his checkbook had gone down with the ship. Fortunately, he had enough on hand to keep the cabdriver interested. He didn't expect to need much more than that.

Their quarry was heading into the city, a fact that worked in their favor, as a cab would be less noticeable in city traffic than if they had headed toward one of the bedroom communities of Long Island.

"So who are we following?" The cabbie asked casually as he kept them two cars back from the white Ford. "Your wife, maybe?"

"Why would you think that?"

"I've had all kinds." The fellow laughed. "You're not the first guy following someone else around. People sure are nosy, aren't they? Well, I figure it's your wife, 'cause why else would you be chasing after some broad with a kid? Get my point? Must be your kid, or you wouldn't want anything to do with it. Right?''

David was depressed by the man's words. More correctly, by the truth in them. The only child he'd ever had any use for in all his life was his own. And, until he'd had that child, he hadn't known that his own son would make him feel differently from the way he did for any other. He should have known that much from the start. He should have known better.

But, no, he'd known less than a New York cabbie when it came to children. And he'd been a fool to even open his mouth on a subject that was so foreign to him. No wonder he'd almost lost his wife for good.

"Hey, you don't want to talk about it, that's fine," the cabbie said when he didn't answer. "I figure, the rate you're paying, we don't need to talk."

"Sorry," David said.

He didn't know how much he wanted to tell the man about the actual situation. It might be best to let him think the woman was his wife, and let it go at it. But, since he didn't know who she would be meeting or what he would have to do later, it might be best to tell him the truth right now. David was finding that the detective business was far more difficult than he'd imagined.

"No," he said at last, "she's not my wife. In fact, she may end up being the wrong person to follow entirely. My son was kidnapped at the airport, and the woman we're following seems to have been involved, providing cover for the kidnappers. I'm hoping she'll lead me to the people responsible."

"A snatch?" The driver whistled tightly. "I should have known it wasn't a woman that had you in a knot."

"Why?"

"Hell, you gave me a C note right off the top. Some guy chasing his wife might promise me a hundred, but I'll bet he'd only give me twenty to start. Most guys having woman trouble are cheap—if you know what I mean."

"Yes, I suppose I know what you mean," David replied, as much to end their conversation as to agree.

"Well, I'll keep on her tail," the man stated. "Don't you worry. I got four kids myself, and I'd pop any bastard harms a hair on their heads. We won't lose her. But if she is the wrong person, and she ends up wanting to sue you for something, then I'm not here. You never got the number of the cab and never asked the guy's name. Right?"

"Right, I won't remember a thing."

That settled, the cabdriver—the name on his license was Dominick Carlotti—concentrated on his driving, with a look of determination on his tanned features. He wasn't about to lose the car when there was a child involved.

The white car they followed moved through Queens without haste and passed through the Queens-Midtown tunnel to Manhattan with Dominick sticking behind admirably. The traffic wasn't as tight as it might have been, so they made good time into the city.

The white car nearly lost them at a light in midtown, but Dominick was able to get a jump on the traffic at the green and swerved to the head of the pack, catching up with the Ford just as they were turning toward the Lower East Side.

When the car finally slowed to a stop, Dominick drove right past them at a moderate speed, as though looking for an address.

"This chick know you?" he asked as he pulled the cab into a slot at the curb.

"She might," David admitted. "I don't know."

"Okay then, you wait a sec." Dominick opened his door and got out of the cab. "I'll see if I can tell where she went. Be right back."

The cabbie tossed his cloth cap on the seat and trotted back toward the door the woman had just entered, while David twisted in his seat to watch him. He was certainly getting his money's worth from this cab ride, but having to continue his passive role in the back seat of the cab was almost more than he could bear.

It seemed hours before Dominick returned to the cab, but when he did, his expression was hopeful.

"She went into a day-care on the first floor." He slipped behind the wheel and turned to look back at David. "There was a sign on the door. City Care for Kids, it says. I figured, what the hell, and I knocked. A big woman answered. Ugly woman, about six-two, with a thick neck like she's been hauling crates all her life." He laughed. "I'd never take my kids to that one, that's for sure."

"Did you see the blond woman inside?"

"Yeah, she was having a cup of coffee and a smoke. I says I'm looking for a place to stash my kid while my wife goes to work, and the weight lifter tells me they're full up. I says okay, thanks anyway, and I'm outta there."

"So what do you think?" David asked. He had come to appreciate this man's judgment. "Does it look like the real thing?"

"Real day-care? No, I don't think so." Dominick scratched his chin and glanced over at the brownstone buildings along the street. "She says they're full, but there were only two kids in there. Most day-cares in the city are full to the rafters. It don't smell right. Besides, this woman ain't the motherly type. She'd never make a living at the business."

"I'd better get in there," David said. "I can't risk that blonde slipping out the back."

"Hold on a sec," Dominick said. "She's having her coffee. The way I see it, she's waiting for someone. It's a day-care, right? Chances are good they'll bring your kid here. Right? I say, give them a couple minutes and see what happens."

"You're probably right," David agreed. "I don't know if I can stand to sit for any length of time, though."

"You'll sit, all right," the other man said. "There's a coffee shop on the corner. We can get a window table and watch from there."

"There's no money for the cab company in your taking a coffee break," David pointed out.

"I own the hack, and the cab company owes me a coffee break, anyway." Dominick laughed, flipping the flag on his meter down. "Besides, I've got to stick around and see how this comes out, don't I? Come on, I'll buy you a cup of joe, mister."

"I never did introduce myself," David said, getting out of the cab. "David Germaine." He extended his hand to shake hands with the driver.

"Dominick Carlotti," the other man said. "Let's go see what kind of Danish they've got."

David's appetite was less than enthusiastic when he took a seat across a table near the front window of Caroline's Coffee and Sweets, across from the building containing the day-care.

"It's in the lower right," Dominick said, pointing out a pair of windows to the right of the stoop. The shades were drawn on both windows.

David commented on the drawn shades. "Doesn't she let any light in for the kids?"

"No, pretty dark. Like I said, I wouldn't send my kid there."

The waitress came by their table, and they both ordered coffee, Dominick taking a couple of pastries, as well. Then they sat watching the building and the street, sat and watched and waited.

"How old is your kid?" Dominick asked.

"What?" David was flustered by the question—suddenly he couldn't remember what Nicole had told him. "About thirteen months," he said. "Yes, a little over a year."

"First child?"

"Yes. Matthew, his name is Matthew."

"A boy just over a year? You're just getting into it." Dominick laughed. "Once they get to walking, you're on the run all day. Then come the 'terrible twos,' when they're not only running and spilling everything, but they're having fits about not getting their way all the time. You'll have a ball."

"If we get him back," David commented, hating himself for even considering the possibility that they might not.

"You'll get him back. You got money, right? So, okay, that's what they want. You pay the ransom, that's all."

"It's not that easy," David said. "They want me to do something for them. If it were just money, I'd have paid long ago."

"So what you gotta do? Kill someone?"

"No, they want me to retrieve something for them. A month ago I said no. I didn't have my son's safety to worry about then."

"So now you do, right. So you do the business for them and you're fine. Is that the picture?"

"Pretty much, on the face of it. I'd do what they want, if I could be certain of my son's safety. But I can't trust them. You see what I mean? I've got to expose them in order to be certain of any future safety at all."

"You've got a problem, that's for sure," Dominick said around a mouthful of pastry. "But what if you're wrong about trusting them? Maybe you can."

"And maybe pigs can fly," David countered.

"You've got a choice? I don't think so. What do they want you to get so badly? It would probably be easier for them to get it themselves than to go to all of this trouble."

"I don't want to go into details," David said. He sipped his coffee and watched the building across the street. No one had gone in or out since the woman had taken the child inside.

"The problem for them is that they don't know where it is. I can find it, and I know how to retrieve it so it isn't damaged. That's why they need me."

"And why they put the grab on your son."

"I should have done what they wanted from the start. I'd have avoided this."

"No, I don't think so," Dominick said, shaking his head. "I think a man's got to live by certain standards. Maybe now the circumstances have changed and you have to bend your own rules, but it sounds like you probably had good reason not to help them at the start. Am I right?"

"I thought so at the time. It's a tangled mess, Dominick, that's for sure. I still don't know what the right thing to do is."

"Save your kid, that's the right thing. Nothing else really matters, does it?"

"No, nothing else does."

They sat in silent agreement for a while, David's eyes rarely leaving the brownstone across from them as the setting sun began to lift a shadow over its face.

"I can't wait much longer," David said after they'd been in the coffee shop for half an hour. "The odds are against them bringing Matthew here."

"Why? If this woman is connected to them, and if the day-care is connected, as well, why wouldn't they bring him?"

"That's an awful lot of ifs," David said sourly. "But I suppose it's the only course of action I have. God, I hate waiting."

"Most people do," Dominick said. "Try driving a hack for a living. You wait for a fare, and then you spend your time driving, waiting for the fare to get out at the end so you can pick up another rider and maybe get a better tip. Everybody is waiting in one way or another.''

"You're quite the philosopher," David commented.

"I got time to philosophize, and plenty of it."

There was no activity across the street for the next fifteen minutes. Then, when David was about ready to take the day-care by force, a gray minivan double-parked before the building and a blond man got out of the passenger side and ran into the building.

David tensed at the table, staring at the van and trying in vain to see through the tinted windows at the rear of the vehicle. He could see movement, but could not make out the identity of the people inside.

"Come on," he said as he dropped a few bills on the table and stood.

"Hey, my treat," Dominick protested.

"Don't worry about it." David was already moving to the door as he spoke.

"Wait. Don't just run out there!" He caught up with David at the door, grabbing his shoulder to stop him.

"Matt might be in that van," David protested.

"And they'll drive off with him in a flash if you barge out there like a mad bull. See what gives first."

"Okay, maybe you're right." David felt as trapped as though he were behind bars as he stood behind the double glass doors of the coffee shop with the other man's restraining hand on his shoulder. "I can't see what's happening."

"Nothing so far... No, wait a second. Yeah, someone is getting out of the rear door."

David could see the crown of a blond head over the van, a woman's long hair blowing in the wind. She was running from the van to the building carrying something... a child!

He threw the door open and emerged running toward the van. The driver saw him coming and opened his door, just stepping out as David reached him. He hit the driver's door with the full weight of his body, slamming it against the man's leg. Then David pulled the door open, sending the howling man sprawling on the street, where he kicked him hard in the ribs without a second thought and ran around the front of the van toward the brownstone.

The scuffle had alerted the others, and the first man looked out of the door briefly as David took the steps two at a time. When David burst through the door, his quarry was just throwing shut the door of the day-care, on the right side of the hall. David followed, hitting the door before anyone could secure it. As he stepped through, however, someone struck him in the face and knocked him back against the wall.

He saw a burst of blue stars and a movement through the haze, and he dropped just an instant ahead of the fist that was returning for a second blow. His assailant struck the wall instead, emitting a high shriek of pain. David kicked out, striking a leg before his head was quite clear enough to see the target.

Then he rolled away, popping up to turn and face the woman who had struck him at the door. She was over six feet tall and built like a linebacker, but her bleeding hand and the kick to the shin had taken the fight out of her, and she just snarled at him and ran out of the door.

"Matt!" he yelled, heading through the front room to the bedrooms. Two children, a girl and a boy about five years old, stood in the short hall, fear etched on their faces.

"Where did the people go?" David asked, throwing open the first door. "The big people. Where did they go?"

"Out back," the girl said, her voice quavering.

"Go out the front," he told them as he continued toward the back of the building. "Go!"

But the first man to enter the house was back, a gun in his hand and a mean look in his eyes as he approached them.

"Hi, mate," he said. "Come on, kiddies, let's take a drive."

"No way." David stepped back, grabbing both children and pulling them forcibly back with him. "They're not going anywhere."

"That's no way to be, mate," the man said. "I've got a responsibility to take care of the little nippers."

"I'll take care of them, as well as my son," David said, still backing up. "You won't get my cooperation while you're still holding my child."

He passed out of the hall and through the kitchen area that lay open to the living room through a food bar. The man stopped at the kitchen door, raising his gun. "Stop," he said with quiet menace.

"Run!" commanded a voice behind them, and David did just that. Turning and snatching up both children, he ran toward the door, where Dominick stood.

A gunshot rang out behind them, but the shot was not aimed at David, but at the cabdriver, who ducked just ahead of the shot and brought his own hand up, holding a revolver. He fired twice as David ran past.

What happened next was hard for David to piece together after the fact. First he heard a low snapping sound, barely noticed as he ran clutching both of his small charges to him. Then came the blast, a hot pressure that propelled them out the front door and down the steps. David's feet flew, but he managed to keep them beneath him until they reached the sidewalk, where he fell, twisting onto his back to avoid harming the children.

Behind them, a second blast shattered the windows of the first-floor apartment, and glass rained down around them as flames licked out through the window frames.

No one else came out of the building, and David was left alone with two sobbing children as the street filled with neighbors gathering in alarm and smoke billowed out of the building.

Chapter Ten

"Nicole, come in here," Jerry called from the office where he'd made his calls earlier. "Quick."

Nicole hurried in to find the scientist watching the television. CNN was tuned in, showing a street scene in chaos.

"What?"

"Listen a second."

The announcer's voice came on after a moment. "To recap the story, gunshots lead to an explosion in Manhattan this afternoon at a neighborhood day-care. Details are sketchy, but police on the scene say that a man rescued two children from the explosion, which ripped through the brownstone structure after a gunman apparently struck a gas line with his bullet. The gunman is reported to have died in the blast, while the hero survived with unannounced injuries. Some witnesses say there may have been a third man involved, but we haven't been able to confirm that with the police. The Good Samaritan, a David Germaine, is being questioned by police at this moment. Further details will be reported as soon as we have them. Back to you, Charles.''

"Unannounced injuries?" Nicole exclaimed in shock. "What does that mean? Where is he? Did they give an address? Anything?"

"Calm down a minute," Jerry said as he picked up the receiver of the telephone. "I can get that from the police precinct. We'll be in touch with David in a minute."

"Calm down?" She stared at Jerry as though he'd just asked her to jump out the window.

He was right, of course, but calmness was out of the question at the moment. Her son was missing, and her husband had been involved in an explosion that had left him injured, and she didn't know how badly he was hurt. With those thoughts in her mind, there was no possibility of calm for Nicole.

MORLEY KRAFT switched off his television after the CNN report and swung his chair around to stare at the bookshelves behind his desk. That damn oceanographer was getting far too much attention. If he weren't holding the trump card just now, he might consider throwing in the towel and looking for another way to save his empire. But there was no turning back from a crime like kidnapping at this stage.

Fortunately, his involvement with the crime was well concealed. And, if the news report was correct, the only man who could have tied him to the incident had died in a convenient explosion in New York. That faceless underling wouldn't be missed at all. Not the way Garth Donnelly was missed. Still, both deaths had helped to keep him safely in the background.

They would never be able to prove a thing against him. It would do no good to gloat now, when skill and care were called for. The oceanographer would get the satellite for him. And then he and his family would have a chance to study the great white shark—up close.

NICOLE SAT ANXIOUSLY in the back of the cab as they sped toward the address given in the television news report. Jerry had stayed behind to complete their arrangements for the ransom, but she wouldn't be satisfied by calling the police in order to get in touch with David. She had to be at his side.

A faint plume of smoke could be seen ahead of them as they began moving south along the avenue, making Nicole even more anxious to hurry. But the rush-hour traffic had set in, and the streets were snarled with drivers trying to get out of town after work or into town for an evening's entertainment. Finally, as they sat stalled in traffic only two blocks away, Nicole paid the fare and got out of the cab to walk the remaining distance to the site.

Walking wasn't much better, of course, but it gave her a sense of motion that she needed just then. David was injured, and she couldn't just passively sit in a cab.

The block itself was barricaded and the street filled with fire trucks and police vehicles. Men were moving about, firemen coiling their hoses now while policemen talked to people from the neighborhood. Nicole paused at the barricade, then slipped past and moved along the front of the building until she came to where the sidewalk was littered with glass.

The smell of smoke hung in the air, a still-acrid sensation. Nicole couldn't see any sign of David in the confusion of uniforms and moving people at the scene of the explosion. Then she spotted the ambulance with a cluster of people around it, and she hurried to the vehicle.

"David!" she cried out, spying him seated in the rear of the ambulance. Faces turned her way, wondering about her connection and whether she should be stopped or allowed through to the man who was the center of attention.

"Nicole!" He turned and jumped down from the vehicle, running to meet her with open arms. "Why are you here?"

"I saw the report on television," she explained, overjoyed to see him whole and healthy and to be within his arms again. "I had to come."

"What about Matt? Did you hear anything?"

"They want a million dollars."

"What?" Confusion twisted his features as he parted from her. "I don't get it."

"We figure that it's a cover," she said. "They don't want the real reason to get out to the cops. Or, more likely, they want the police to disbelieve you if you do tell them. After all, why would they ask for money if they want a service?"

"Crafty, aren't they?"

"Excuse me, but does this woman have some bearing on events here?" A stout fellow in a gray suit spoke up, official concern stamping his features with a perpetual scowl.

"This is my wife, Nicole," David told him. "This is Detective Trent, dear," he said to Nicole.

"You mention a ransom?" the detective asked. "Have you reported the demand?"

"Not yet. I saw the report of the explosion on the news and came right here. David's partner is at our apartment now working out the money arrangement."

"Your husband told us about an Australian wanting information from him. Are you assuming that the ransom demand came from him?"

"Yes, I think so," she told the officer.

"Which would mean that he is connected to this day-care operation," the man mused.

"Day-care? I don't understand." Nicole looked to David. "The news report didn't give any details."

"I'm pretty certain I saw the woman who took Matthew come into this building," David told her. "The apartment she went into was advertised as a day-care business."

"Did she take our son into the blast?"

"I don't know. She was carrying a child, but I couldn't see who it was. Don't worry," he assured her, "they were out the back before the explosion. Probably a block away by then."

"How did it happen? The report mentioned gunfire."

"I'm not clear on it. There was a cabdriver—a guy named Dominick—who went in with me. He shot at the other man, and there was an explosion. I was on my way out the door by that time."

"And the children? There was a mention of children on television."

"Two kids," he said. "They've been taken away already. I guess they were the only two children in the day-care."

"If it was a day-care." The policeman scowled. "We've got a backlog of citations and violations against it. Child welfare officers have it on their watch list."

"And Morley Kraft is connected to them?" Nicole asked.

"Probably not in any way that we can prove," David said. "But he must be connected, because I saw the woman come in here."

"And you chased them unarmed? David, you could have been killed going after them like that."

"I wasn't alone, though," he said, then turned to the detective. "What about Dominick? No one has said anything about him."

"I don't know what to say." The policeman shrugged. "There's only one body in the apartment, and he was in the kitchen. You said your cabbie was by the front door."

"Right. It was the other man in the kitchen."

"Then your cabbie took off for some reason."

"How could he have done that? The cab is still parked at the curb, just down the block."

"We're checking on that. Bertini!" he called to a man talking with a pair of uniformed officers. "Anything on the cab yet?"

"The hack is registered to Alvin Petricka, and the cab company says he called in sick today."

"Not Dominick Carlotti?"

"No, Petricka. We haven't talked to him yet."

"Maybe this Carlotti guy was in on the snatch, too," Detective Trent said.

"Why would he take me to his own people? He could have easily lost the car in traffic and left me hanging. And he had a cabdriver's license posted in the car."

"I don't have any answers yet, Mr. Germaine. All I can do is keep checking."

"Okay, well, is that all you need from me?"

"Yes, sir, you can go now. I've got your number, and will get ahold of you if I need to."

"Good. I'll be in town for a while, anyway," David told him. "I'll call if I have to leave."

"Yeah, well, good luck with your son," the man said as he extended his hand. "Hang in there."

"We will."

When the policeman turned back to his duties, David took Nicole's hand in his and held it tightly. "You have a ransom demand?" he asked. "What's the arrangement?"

"Tonight at nine o'clock, in Central Park," she said. "We're supposed to bring the money, but there were no other details."

"The kidnapping couldn't be unrelated, could it?" David asked.

"Jerry doesn't think it could be," Nicole said as they began to walk swiftly along the street, away from the blast scene. "How are you? The news report said you were injured."

"A bump on the head," he said, laughing. "That's my second explosion in as many days. I'm getting to be an old hand at this."

"What about the children?"

"Nobody knows who their parents are. The neighbors don't remember anyone dropping off kids for care for quite some time. They thought the day-care was closed."

"Couldn't the children tell the police who their parents were?"

"I imagine they can, but they were so scared that neither one of them could say much." They turned the corner and left the confusion of the crime scene as they made their way north, looking for a cab. "The authorities will straighten that out, I'm sure. Dominick was right about that place, though." David laughed. "I sure wouldn't bring any kid of mine to stay there."

"Dominick was your disappearing cabdriver?"

"Yes. I can't explain him, Nicole, and that bothers me." David was more bothered than he even wanted to admit to himself. He had found that he liked the straightforward cabbie, and he hated to harbor any unkind thoughts about the man. Still, he'd been armed, and he'd disappeared after the explosion. There was no explanation for that.

"Well . . ." Nicole began, pondering the same question. "It's not exactly unheard-of for a cabbie to be armed in this city. He probably always has that."

"Sure, but where is he? And why was he driving someone else's cab? Those are the bothersome questions. I just don't have any answers for them."

"If Morley Kraft has a Lower East Side day-care working for him, there's no reason to think he couldn't have a cabbie or two on the payroll, as well," Nicole reasoned.

"Which brings us back to the question of why he helped me find the day-care. That makes no sense."

"Unless the kidnapping was unrelated," she said as David stepped to the curb to hail an approaching cab. "Maybe your friend Dominick was sent by Kraft to follow us, and the kidnapping was as much of a surprise to him as it was to us."

"You're right," David said. The cab stopped, and he opened the rear door and helped Nicole in, sliding in beside her as he gave the cabbie the address. "I never considered that there might be more than one group out to get the satellite."

"One of Kraft's clients, maybe," she said. "I imagine he plans to charge a steep price for the technology in that satellite. They'd probably rather just cut out the middleman."

"So there could be any number of interested parties out there, couldn't there?"

"This is getting more complicated by the minute."

"Let's just hope the ransom payoff gets Matthew back," David said. "Taking our son from the middle of a crowded airport like that was probably his best possible demonstration of his ability to get us. I'm sure that's all he wants it to be."

"Sure, but a million-dollar ransom?"

"Like you said, it's probably a cover. It has to look like a real kidnapping to the police," David said. "Don't worry, we'll have Matt back by nine-thirty."

"Oh, David, I hope you're right."

Still, Nicole couldn't help but feel that he wasn't right, and that things were going to get a lot worse before they had any chance of seeing their son again.

THE RED LIGHT of the setting sun was nearly spent by the time they had the money together in a suitcase and ready for a stroll through the park. The police had consented to remain in the background, knowing from experience that they could little affect the outcome of a ransom payment by surveillance. Just before Nicole and David left for the park, however, the police treated the money with a special dye to mark the fingers of anyone who handled the money within the next few hours so that they would show purple stains under ultraviolet light.

Husband and wife stood side by side, love for their absent child bringing them together again. But neither of them wanted to talk about the issue at hand, or what they would do if their plan failed.

"You're not going to be too close, are you?" David asked one of the FBI officers who had prepared their case of money. "We can't afford to have you be seen."

"We've done this before," the man replied tersely. "It's better to lose the money than the child, and I'd rather never catch these people than bungle the job."

"I'm sure they know what they're doing," Nicole said. Her nerves were so taut that it seemed to hurt her deep inside even to speak; she just wanted everyone to be quiet for a few moments before they were on their way.

"I didn't say they didn't know what they were doing," David said, his own nervousness showing in his constant shifting from foot to foot as he spoke. "But we're talking about my son here. I just want to be certain."

"*Our* son," Nicole countered.

"Yes, our son," he answered. "I didn't mean anything by that."

"No, but you have become awfully possessive about him."

"Well, should I be? You're the one who—"

"Relax, gang." Jerry stopped their budding argument with calm force. "His and hers and ours and whatever don't matter much right now, do they? You're both on edge, so try to relax."

"Right," Nicole said. "I'm nervous as a cat."

"God, Nicole, I can't stand even thinking of what might happen," David said. "I feel just sick."

"Me too," she said. And she slipped her arm around his waist and rested her head against his chest, taking solace in the steady beating of his heart while he held her to him in a protective embrace.

His presence almost made her feel better. She felt that it would be impossible for God to allow anything bad to happen to their son just as the family was coming together again.

But then, Morley Kraft wasn't God, and nothing good had come from their short association with him.

MORLEY KRAFT was well beyond the reach of the law-enforcement personnel who were preparing to trap his underlings that night. He was safely at sea, just beyond the U.S. territorial limits, as an unlisted passenger aboard his corporate yacht, *Gambler's Luck*. The vessel had been at sea since his financial troubles began, staying away from the possibility of seizure by the authorities, should his creditors decide to stop waiting and call in his loans.

He had always rather liked the ship, preferring the swelling motion of the sea to the static feeling of solid ground beneath his feet. Morley was the type of man who could never sit still, either physically or financially, and he came close to relaxing only while on the yacht.

"If I lose everything in the world," he had once vowed to Garth Donnelly, "this boat will be the last thing to go."

Now, as the sun settled down beyond the American mainland, he stood at the rail of the ship with a glass of brandy in his hand and watched the Atlantic Ocean roll beneath him. He wondered if everything was going according to plan, but was only vaguely concerned.

The people he'd hired to snatch the kid were expendable. They were low-life baby thieves who had operated an adoption racket from the shoddy apartment that someone had managed to blow up that afternoon. The only one of the group who might possibly have managed to figure out who had hired them to steal the boy had died in the blast. Morley had no connection to any of the rest of them.

Let the cops have them; they were scum, anyway.

Morley felt certain that Germaine had gotten the point by now. Unless he complied with his wishes, Germaine would never be certain of his safety or the safety of his family. Never.

And if Kraft's empire fell to ruin because of the scientist's stubborn honesty, he would make certain that Germaine paid a steep price. There was very little time left for him to do the smart thing. Very little time indeed.

DAVID WAS PREPARING to do the "smart thing" even as Morley Kraft watched the distant shore from his boat. He and Nicole had left the apartment with the briefcase of money shortly after the FBI agents left out the back of the building. It was 8:45 p.m., and they walked with deliberate casualness from the building across to the park, while keeping a wary eye out for trouble.

Nicole had never expected to be carrying a million dollars in a case, let alone carrying such a sum into Central Park after dark. It seemed to her that the kidnappers hadn't planned this caper with a lot of common sense. Nicole and David might be robbed en route to the drop-off, or the kidnappers themselves might be robbed of the money after they got it. A lot of things could happen at night in a big-city park.

It seemed as though they were the only ones about at the moment, however. The sound of their footsteps on the concrete paths brought scraping echoes back to them, like the ghosts of past strollers taking the air at night. Aside from a few nocturnal animals, they neither saw nor heard any other life.

"If I had known it was this peaceful in the park at night, I'd have come here walking before," David said, a hint of forced humor in his voice.

"This whole thing gives me the willies," Nicole admitted. "What if we're robbed?"

"We won't be," he assured her. "The park isn't really packed full of criminals after dark. It only seems that way."

"Just part of the city's charming image, right?"

"Yeah, something like that."

They fell silent again, walking slowly along a path to Cleopatra's Needle and then north, waiting for some sign from their son's captors.

"I hope I didn't mess things up this afternoon," David said grimly. "Maybe they think I double-crossed them by hunting them down."

"No, there wouldn't have been time for you to get to them if you were at the apartment to receive the message," she said. "Even they should know that."

But she couldn't be certain of what they would know, could she? It was possible that the kidnappers would hold off and make them wait another day before completing their deal. Maybe this was just a run-through so that they could look for police interference. She couldn't know.

All she could do was to walk through the park, feeling as though her every move were being scrutinized. She hated the spooky feeling of eyes watching from the shadows, even though she sincerely hoped they were watching right now. Her son's life depended upon his captors watching them and believing that they had not gone to the police.

An owl hooted and rustled into flight from the branch of a nearby tree, and Nicole jumped at the sound. The hair on the back of her neck stood on end as she looked around, trying to see the night hunter after its prey. The parallel between themselves and the unfortunate rodent the owl finally caught was all too obvious. She and David were being stalked by night hunters, too. She could only hope their fate would be more benign.

She thought she heard someone clear his throat in the distance. That, or a thousand other sounds that her anxious ears might have translated into the sound of someone out there—someone waiting in the dark.

"Why don't they do something?"

"I don't know." The strain of the night was clear in David's voice. "You didn't miss anything in the instructions, did you?"

"No, neither Jerry nor I missed anything," she said. "And the cops checked it over, too."

"Don't say that," he whispered quickly. "Not so loud, anyway."

"Sorry." Nicole fought to avoid looking around, hoping that the kidnappers weren't close enough to hear them talk, but feeling in her heart that they must be. *What if they heard you, and they're not going to go through with it now?* She couldn't bear to think like that. She had to try maintaining a positive outlook, or she would simply collapse in terror.

"Where the hell are they?" David said.

Nicole said nothing, for there was nothing to say, no topic of conversation that might be safely followed that night.

A shadow passed over the moon. The owl was hunting overhead.

And then the sound of their hunters came clearly to Nicole's ears. Someone had stepped on a twig, taking care to be unseen, but no longer caring about quiet. Someone wanted to be heard.

David had heard the sound, too, and he tensed beside her. Still, they continued walking north through the park, while waiting for the kidnappers to make the next move.

Their wait was suddenly over. A man stepped onto the sidewalk, about twenty-five feet ahead of them. He was dressed in dark clothing and wearing a hat; his hands were apparently empty.

"The case," he said. "Put it down right there."

"Where's my son?" David didn't move to comply, but stood his ground beside Nicole.

"Safe." The man stepped nearer, pointing to the ground at David's feet. "Put it right there."

"Where is he?"

"Near at hand." The man waited, his face shadowed by the large brim of his hat. "Now put the damn case down and back away."

"I want to see my son!" David snapped.

Nicole grasped his arm, trying to stop him from doing anything rash just then. But, even as she moved, she caught sight of a movement behind them and heard the running steps approaching.

"David!" she cried out, too late.

The second person swung something hard against the back of David's head, knocking him to the ground. Nicole instinctively grabbed at the hand holding the club as it swung past her, diving on the dark-clad figure and trying to pull his stocking cap from his head.

The attacker stumbled, twisting in Nicole's grasp as the cap was pulled askew and blond hair cascaded out of it. It was the woman from the airport!

Nicole tried to hold her more tightly now, but the woman threw her off, kicking out at her when she tried to close in again. David was on his feet again by then, and met the first man head-on as he grabbed the case of money. For a second, the parties froze, Nicole and the blond woman facing each other, about five feet apart, and David holding the man by both shoulders and staring into his eyes.

"When do we get our son?" David snarled at the man.

But the man made no reply. He only spun, slamming the case against the side of David's head and twisting free to run with his companion and be swallowed by the darkness once more.

"Dammit!" David shouted, bending to rest both hands on his knees and catch his breath.

Nicole stood staring at the shadows within the trees where the two had disappeared. The park was quiet again, as though they had never been there at all.

But in the distance she heard the cry of the owl as he caught his prey.

Chapter Eleven

"They let you take quite a walk through the park before they finally made contact." Special Agent Adam Hardin was scowling and pacing, and it looked as though he had been doing both for quite some time before Nicole and David got back to the apartment. "We expected them to make contact sooner."

"Is that an excuse for losing them?" David asked angrily.

He had thrown his jacket across the room upon entering the apartment, where Jerry and the agent had been waiting, walked immediately across to the liquor cabinet, only to slam it shut and stalk to the kitchen to pour himself a cup of coffee.

"We don't know that we have lost them," Hardin said, with forced calmness. "I haven't heard from all of our agents yet."

"If they had lost the people, you probably would have heard by now, wouldn't you?" Nicole forced herself to be hopeful and look for the best interpretation she could find for the situation. Still, in her heart, she agreed with David. The FBI had probably lost them.

"Yes, I would have."

"If anything happens to Matthew, I'll . . ."

"You'll what, Mr. Germaine?" Hardin cut in. "How could you have done anything differently without us? You'd have had no chance at all of following them alone, and you know that. Hell, man, we had to stay far enough back that they wouldn't see us. It wasn't a perfect scenario, but it was a damn sight better than any alternative."

"I'm not disagreeing," David said. "I've just got to blame somebody, and you're handy."

"Nobody told you to fight with them," the agent said. "When a kidnapper says to put the case down and walk away, it's usually best to do just that."

"I didn't fight with them! They attacked me!"

"It was obvious that you were stalling."

"I just wanted some assurance that Matt was all right."

"What kind of assurance did you expect to get? Nothing that you could believe. No, the only assurance you want is to have him back, and you don't get that by making it look as if you're trying to drag things out."

"Gentlemen, stop it," Nicole put in. "This is getting us nowhere. As I see it, all we can do now is wait for a call. I think everything has gone as well as it could, so far."

David frowned and tasted his coffee. It was bitter, but it matched his mood. But what right did he have to be this way? Nicole was remaining calm, wasn't she? Lord knew she must be about ready to burst, yet she was keeping her head. It was remarkable, when he thought of it. Of course, she managed a lot of control when it came to Matthew, didn't she? She hadn't given in to any random urges to inform him of his parentage—assuming that she'd had any—and if she had, they might not be in this fix right now.

No, stop that. How can you get on with your life if every thought brings you full circle to blaming Nicole again? You have to get over it.

Looking at Nicole, seeing her face set in determined hopefulness, even as a hint of despair lurked in her hazel eyes, he couldn't help but feel a deep and abiding love for her. She was his love, his wife, the mother of his son. His son! He had a son!

He knew as he looked at her that he loved them both more than he could ever love anything else in his life. They were everything to him. All he had to do now was to learn how to express his love.

As a start, he put down his coffee cup and walked over to slip his arm around Nicole's shoulder. "It'll be all right," he said. "Don't worry."

"I'll try not to," Nicole said. "But it looks like worrying is the only thing we've got to do."

It felt good to have his arm around her. It reassured her, when nothing else could have. There had been a distance between them since her return that hurt her. Since their initial lusty rushing together, the pain of their situation had driven them apart. Now the pain of Matthew's abduction seemed to be bringing them together again. Maybe something good would come of this, after all.

They waited for another half hour before the remaining agents reported in. As David had predicted, they had lost the kidnappers shortly after they left the park. It seemed that their last hope had gone. They could only wait for their next set of instructions.

"What about that cabdriver?" David asked. "Anything?"

"Dominick Carlotti has a valid hack license," Hardin replied as he got his jacket and prepared to leave. "But his listed address was torn down a year ago. Petricka, the guy who owns the cab he was driving, said that Carlotti worked for the company a year or more back. He wanted to earn a few extra bucks today, so Petricka loaned it to him out of friendship and took a day off."

"Do you think he was waiting for me, then?"

"It looks that way, though we have no idea why. If he was in on the kidnapping, there was no point in taking you right to them. But if he wasn't in on it, why was he there at all?"

"Yes, why indeed?" David said thoughtfully. He hadn't a clue. All he knew was that the man had helped him—possibly even saved his life—and he didn't know why.

"We'll be on top of any call you get," Agent Hardin said as he left the apartment. "Tracing calls these days is as easy as breathing, so they can't give us the slip. Don't stall or try to drag out the conversation. Just agree with whatever they want. Right?"

"Right," Nicole said. David remained silent.

"Don't worry," he told her. "If they're smart enough to pull off a snatch like this one, then you can be sure they're smart enough to know the consequences of harming the child. They don't want to hurt him.''

"Right," she agreed, knowing that not wanting to cause harm wouldn't necessarily stop them from causing it. "Good night."

"I'll be off, too," Jerry said when the door had closed behind the agent. "Unless you want me to stay and help you pace."

"No, go ahead," David said. "Thanks for everything."

"Hell, what are partners for, anyway?" He left them with a hopeful smile.

Silence seemed to invade the apartment like an occupying army as the two people remaining stood awkwardly, unable to find words of encouragement for each other.

"I have to take a shower," Nicole said at last. "I feel incredibly dirty."

"I'll stand guard over the phone," David said, looking at the instrument as he did, as though daring it to ring. "They're probably still driving around, making sure nobody is following them."

"Yes, you're right. They'll call when they know it's safe."

"Right."

They both felt empty and devoid of the energy needed to continue a conversation. It was just too much work to talk, so they would find other things to do for the time being, and hope this period of enervation would pass.

Their entire future hung on one phone call.

IN THE PARK across from the apartment, the man calling himself Dominick Carlotti watched with binoculars. He had been there for about fifteen minutes, having arrived before Agent Hardin left for the night, and he was watching intently now.

Draw the blinds, for crying out loud, he thought, scowling. People in upper-floor apartments seemed to think they were invisible. From this distance and elevation, however, Dominick could see quite a bit inside the apartment. This was the very spot the kidnappers had watched from, earlier. Dominick had been watching them.

He saw Nicole leave the room, and a light came on in a smaller window, over from the living room. *Bathroom. At least that shade is down.*

David stood looking toward where the woman had gone for a moment. He took a couple of steps in that direction, then stopped and turned and looked at the phone for a long time. Finally he walked out of the room.

Another light came on. The curtains were drawn over that window, however.

It figures that the only uncovered windows are the ones that should be covered. He shook his head, wondering just who was in charge of training FBI agents these days.

After making certain that they weren't planning to leave the apartment, Dominick turned and walked back toward the street. He got into a red Le Baron convertible and drove away.

Nearly an hour later, he stopped at the curb before a small house in Queens and sat looking at the structure for a moment. It needed paint, and it stood out in the street of well-tended houses.

They might as well hang out a sign saying Kidnappers Live Here, he thought. It was best to be done with these people.

Dominick got out of the car and hurried up the walk to the house. He rang the bell and then knocked impatiently on the door. After a moment, a blond woman answered.

"Danny! Yeah, come on in!" she shouted, drunkenly. "God, we did it! What a haul!"

"Yes, you did it," he said, smiling tightly. "So where's the kid?"

"In the other room. I think he's sleeping."

"You think he is?" Dominick laughed. "Boy, you're loaded with motherly instincts, aren't you?"

"Don't give her grief." A man entered the room from the kitchen, carrying two bottles of beer. "She did all right with the little brat. Here, have a beer. Celebrate awhile."

Dominick dismissed the offered beverage. "I'm driving. I came to pick up the kid."

"What? How come?" the man asked.

"He's got to go back eventually, you know," Dominick said. "You weren't planning on keeping him?"

"He's a cute kid," the woman said. "We figured he'd be worth ten grand more."

"No, not this one." Dominick shook his head in remonstration. "You'll have to settle for a million in cash."

"Why?" she asked. "Hey, I don't like you coming here, telling us our business."

"I don't care if you like it. You were put on to this sweet deal for a specific reason, and you won't be allowed to screw it up by changing the plan."

"Or what?"

"Or you won't wake up tomorrow morning." Dominick spoke evenly and with complete sincerity. If it were up to him, people like this would be shot on general principle. "Now bundle up Junior for me and I'll get out of your hair. You can all get drunk and fall over each other, and we won't have to worry about the kid while you're doing it."

"That's a pretty high-toned attitude," the man said. "Dave was killed today, you know. I think we deserve a little extra consideration for the loss."

"You get a bigger cut of the million now, don't you? That's consideration enough. Get the kid."

"Yeah, the hell with him, Charlie," the woman said. "I don't like his bossy attitude, anyway. Get the little brat out of here."

Charlie left the room, leaving Dominick and the woman staring at each other in open contempt. After a moment, he brought Matthew out and handed him unceremoniously over to Dominick.

"Hey, little nipper," Dominick said. "How's it going? Did they remember to feed you?"

Matthew yawned, rubbing his eyes as he looked up at the new man who was holding him. He studied Dominick's face closely, as though memorizing it, and then he smiled. He had decided that he liked this man.

"Good night," Dominick said. He turned and left the house without another word.

Dominick had already strapped a car seat into the back seat of the Le Baron, and he secured Matthew in it before driving away.

"Okay, little Matt," Dominick said as he picked up the receiver of his car phone and dialed a number. "Here's where they get theirs."

After a couple rings, his call was answered, and he said, "Yeah, I know where you can find some kidnappers. Guys put the snatch on an oceanographer's kid. Germaine. David Germaine. They're in a house in Queens with the ransom money. The kid isn't there anymore, so you don't have to be too careful. Me? No, I don't want to leave my name."

But he did leave them the address of the house from which he had just driven away, and he was grinning when he hung up the receiver.

"Okay, Junior," he said. "We've got some errands to run. Then maybe you and me will go out for a few beers. What you say, Matt?"

Matthew laughed and tugged at the straps holding him into his chair. He didn't know where he was going, but it looked interesting so far.

DAVID PICKED UP the baby book from his desk and looked at it. There was a slight stain from salt water on the cover, and he brushed away the slight crust of salt left on that patch. He opened the book, working his mouth silently as though about to say something, but letting it go at a pensive smile.

It hurt to look at the pictures and read the information kept inside the book. His son's size and weight at birth. His first tooth, first word, first everything.

There was Matthew, smiling out of a plastic tub, his hair plastered down on his small head. From the puddles on the table where the tub was sitting, it looked as though he had done quite a bit of splashing before the picture. Couldn't keep still, could he?

He was a natural in the water.

Matthew in his sleeper, with a brown teddy bear.

Did he have the bear with him now? No, they hadn't salvaged it from the apartment. They wouldn't even have this book, if Nicole hadn't been foolish enough to return for it.

Matthew in his crib, holding the bars, like a gleeful convict shouting at the warden. Such a happy child. David realized that he had never seen the child unhappy, except when he and Nicole argued. He vowed never to argue in front of Matt again, for the thought of making his child unhappy chilled him to the bone.

David turned through the pages slowly, savoring every image of his son. Occasionally there were shots of Matthew with his mother, the two of them looking perfect together, a perfect family image. Who had taken those pictures? Who was it that had shared those beautiful moments while he was in limbo, cast out by ignorance of his own unwillingness to interfere with Nicole's private goal.

He hadn't wanted to bully her, had he? Wasn't he behaving like a perfect New Age male by letting her have that freedom? Wasn't that what he was supposed to do?

If he had only behaved more like a caveman and less like a man of the world, he wouldn't have missed that time with his son. It was clear to him now that ignorance was not bliss.

David closed the book and then carried it and the videotape over to his television. He slipped the tape into the VCR and turned on the TV and sat before it on the couch as an image came on the screen.

"Oh, so nice. Such a nice boy." Nicole was speaking, apparently holding the camcorder over Matt's crib, as the child blinked up at her, confused about what Mommy was doing. He was wearing a fluffy blue sleeper with a lamb stitched on the chest, to the left of the zipper. His hair was fine and thin, a crown of corn silk shimmering in the light.

"Can you smile for the camera?" Nicole asked. "Smile for Mommy."

Matthew was having none of that smile business, though he seemed content enough to watch his mother manipulate the camcorder.

"Can the big boy smile?"

No, his lower lip twitched and pouted out, and Matthew began to cry.

The scene changed abruptly, saving David the heartache of watching his son cry. He was in the little plastic tub, splashing gleefully in the water. It was the same setting as the photograph from the book, clearly shot before that picture was taken.

"Cheee!" Matt shouted and splashed. "Chee ga!" The water splattered the table and his face equally, and he laughed heartily at the results of his splashing.

David couldn't tell how old he was here. He lacked the personal experience to tell a baby's age. But Matt was able to sit and—as he showed a moment later—quite able to crawl out of that little tub.

The camera jiggled a bit; apparently Nicole had put it on a tripod, for she slipped into the shot next to bathe her son.

Nicole was heavier in this picture than she was now, not fat, but still showing the latent signs of the pregnancy she'd just completed. She smiled briefly at the camera and then began to move a cloth over Matt's pudgy little body.

"Oh, such a big man," she said to the child as she washed him. "Such a big swimmer. Are you going to be a swimming boy when you get bigger? Going to be like..." But she didn't finish that, and she quickly changed her tone. "Come on, darling, let's get you dry. No, wait a second—" she amended, stepped out of the shot again. "Let Mommy get the camera first. You're such a cute little swimmer, we've got to put it in your book."

There was a flash, and the photograph in the baby album was completed, giving David a feeling of almost having been there for that one event in his son's life. Almost.

David swallowed hard, blinking. He felt as though his heart were encased in stone, a binding of concrete that made each pulse painful and heavy. He could barely breathe against the stone in his chest, and it seemed that the only way to lessen the pressure was to dribble the stone away in tears.

He wiped the back of his hand over his cheeks, sniffing back the emotion, while his son began walking on the screen before him.

Obviously this wasn't his first attempt to walk. Still, David watched with painful pride as Matthew took a step and fell back on his diapered bottom, a surprised expression lighting his eyes. The boy laughed and pulled himself up against the arm of an overstuffed couch. Then, arms out like a tightrope walker, he tried it again. Two steps, three, then down, laughing.

David sat forward a bit in the couch, straining to help Matt walk as a tear trickled down his cheek. "Come on," he whispered. "You can make it."

Matthew walked five steps on his next try, and he didn't fall, but grabbed the couch for support and lowered himself to the floor so that he might make faster progress on his hands and knees. That was enough walking for one day.

In the next scene, he had the hang of it, more or less, and tottered from the couch to a chair and out to the kitchen table without falling once. David felt immeasurably proud of his son's accomplishment. Those were his first few steps on the road of life, and he was taking them in stride.

David used the remote to turn off the VCR and turned down the sound of the show that came on in place of his son's smiling face. He sat quietly in the silent room for a moment, watching the moving images on the screen, without seeing them. What a beautiful child. How could he ever have said he didn't want children? While he had meant that he didn't want children *just then*, rather than *ever*, he had said the offending words nonetheless. Maybe Nicole had overreacted, but she had had cause.

He dried his eyes on his shirtsleeves and cleared his throat, trying to remove the obstruction of emotion still holding him. But the mingled feelings of love and loss, pride and anxiety, couldn't be pushed aside. He felt that he might always be short of breath because of it.

The damp scent of soap and shampoo wafted slowly through the room around him as he sat, making him aware of Nicole's presence before he heard her at the door of his den. He turned on the couch and looked back at her, leaning against the door frame in her own robe, wearing her fuzzy slippers and a towel wrapped around her head. She looked like a miracle standing there, a sight he'd thought he'd never see again.

"I'm sorry," she said quietly. Her frown darkened her features a bit, making the constriction in David's throat worse.

"I, uh, I'm supposed to say that," he said, clearing his throat again. "I am sorry."

She shrugged. "Maybe we both should."

"Come here," David said. "I've missed you."

Nicole walked around and sat in the space he made beside him, within his extended arm. His arm felt good around her; it took away the chill of the dampness left by her shower. She laid her head against his shoulder, angling the towel back away from his face.

"I should have come after you at the start," he said. "Instead of following my instincts, I tried to be logical. I counted to ten, and then I let you have your space."

"I was hoping you would come for me," she admitted. "Not at first, of course. No, I just wanted to get away and let you know what you were missing without me. Later, I just didn't have the courage to admit what I'd done to you."

"You did what I said I wanted," he said bitterly. "You made it so that I didn't have a child to contend with on the ship. I guess we both got what we thought we wanted at the time."

"Can you forgive me?" Bitter regret clutched at Nicole's heart, making her breath seem filled with powder in her chest.

"Forgive you?" David sighed, tightening his arm around her. "I can't blame you—not really—so forgiveness doesn't really enter into it."

"Surely you blame me," she said.

"When I think about it too much, and I let my mind wander back to what might have been, I get angry," he admitted. "I feel so mad that I want to beat my head against the wall. But it's just—well, I don't know if I can explain it—it's more a formless anger than anger against you. I missed so much, and it tees me off, but it seems like my own damn fault. God, Nicole, I feel so much more grateful about having you back than I do angry about your leaving that I just can't blame you."

"I blame me."

"Don't." He kissed her forehead lightly, nuzzling it with his lips. "I think that, rather than forgiveness, we need to just get over it. It's done now."

"I missed you, too." She returned his kiss with her own on the firm flesh of his jaw, just before his ear.

The stubble of his beard tickled her nose. "God, how I missed you," she said, lifting her face to look into his eyes.

He brought his lips down to hers, holding them tenderly in the kiss as his tongue moistened them.

Nicole's heart pounded, her body flushing with love and desire in her husband's embrace. He held her so tenderly, like a delicate flower he was afraid he might crush with too much emotion, like a dream from which he was afraid of waking. She welcomed his kisses, pulling the towel from her hair and throwing it aside as she kissed him in return. His love was the only possible balm to her anxiety, the only drug that could soothe her now.

She loosened the tie of her robe, inviting his hand in to slip over her heated flesh. It moved tenderly on her, cupping her breast carefully, his thumb moving briefly in that well-remembered circular motion before moving around her back to pull her closer to him. His hand grasped her bottom, holding her firmly as she shrugged the robe away from her outer arm and brought her hand up to his face—still maintaining their kiss.

"I missed those hands," she whispered, pushing him back lightly. "No, wait," she told him, when he tried to sit up. "I'll just get a few things out of the way."

She stood and dropped her robe to the floor and then knelt naked on the couch beside him to unbutton his shirt and open it to her loving caresses. His skin was hot, and she slipped her cheek over the light hair that adorned his muscular chest as she pulled his shirt free and tugged at the buckle of his belt.

In a moment, Nicole had freed him from his slacks and held him as she brought her lips back to his with a possessive kiss. She straddled her husband, rocking herself slowly down to his lap, where she sat still, while he found her nipples with his lips and brought her ardor to full flame.

They sat unmoving for a long time. Nicole held his head to her breast, her arms around his head and shoulders and his around her back as they sat in quiet union and didn't say a word. Then Nicole allowed her eager body to rock slightly, moving herself on him until the glow within her grew bright and hot and burst through her in a rush.

David gasped then, his body tensing just as hers tightened in orgasm, and his release was a new heat within her. A new burst of love.

She lay against him, holding on to the feeling of him as happy tears flowed down her cheeks. She was home once more. She was home.

But her brief respite from fear for her son was over, and her thoughts slipped back to him as her body relaxed into the soothing afterglow of her love. She was home; Matthew wasn't. Would he ever be?

"He'll be all right," David said, sensing her thoughts. "They don't dare hurt him."

"I want to believe that," Nicole whispered. "I really do."

"The last thing on earth Morley Kraft wants is . . . Wait." He tensed, and then he lifted her gently but quickly from him and grabbed the remote control to raise the volume on the television.

"It was a tip from an anonymous informant that led police to this location to begin with," a woman was saying on-screen. Behind her, flames were licking at the windows of a rather nondescript house somewhere in the city.

"What is it?" Nicole sat on the front of the couch, feeling for the robe on the floor while keeping her eyes on the TV.

"I don't know," he said, securing his belt. "They just had a picture of a woman on the screen. It looked like the one who grabbed Matt at the airport."

"God, no!" Nicole gasped. "What happened there?"

"Listen," he said, nodding toward the set.

"Police surrounded the house and called for the suspects to come out," the reporter said. "When they refused, tear gas was used to force them out. That was apparently when the fire started, and it rushed through the structure quickly. Kitty Stevens, a convicted felon, emerged with a weapon and was shot dead by police outside. Her partner tried to escape out the back, with what is believed to be a briefcase filled with money. A third man died from smoke inhalation before firemen could get him out."

A grainy photograph came on the screen again, and Nicole cried out in alarm.

"Yes, that's her! Oh, David, where's Matt? He couldn't have been in there, could he? God, David, he couldn't have been!"

"They haven't mentioned him yet," David said hopefully. He felt like throwing up as he watched, a feeling of absolute fear gripping him as the reporter continued with her report.

"Apparently the three were celebrating in the house, and the dead man is reported to have been passed out on the couch when the fire started. No other deaths or injuries have been reported. We spoke to a law-enforcement official moments ago."

The report cut to videotape of the reporter standing with a man who was looking back toward the house, where flames were burning much more brightly. "I know you're busy," the reporter said, "but could you tell us what the purpose of the police raid was this evening? What happened?"

"We received a tip that wanted felons were in this house." The man turned to face her as he spoke. It was Agent Hardin. "They wouldn't come out when police called for their surrender, so steps were taken to force them out. I'm not sure how the fire started," he said grimly. "But tear gas canisters can start fires, under the right circumstances."

"I understand that you are not with the New York police force, but are a special agent with the FBI," she said. "What is your connection?"

"I don't want to go into details," he said. He lifted his hand slightly, showing that he was holding David's briefcase in it.

"What about the gas? Did the police overreact?"

"No," he said. "Police responded before I was informed, but I can't find any fault with their actions here. There's a time element involved in the case that precluded negotiation. It's unfortunate that the woman chose to try shooting her way out, but it was her choice."

"If they were drinking, it's possible she wasn't thinking very clearly."

"Possible. But that was her choice, as well."

"How many people were in the house?"

"Three," he said definitely.

"Nobody else was overcome by the blaze?"

"No." He spoke very precisely and purposefully, as though knowing that Nicole and David would be watching. "Nobody else was in the house but the three suspects. We are absolutely certain of that. I've got to go now. Sorry." He hurried off before she could ask him any more questions.

The tape stopped, and the picture of the reporter standing at the scene came back on. "That was Special Agent Hardin of the FBI we spoke to a few minutes ago. Since speaking to him, I've received word that the people in the house were wanted for kidnapping. The case Agent Hardin was holding was apparently the one the suspect tried to take out the back of the house earlier. It is reported to have held a sum of ransom money paid to the three people in the house. As I say, we don't have any confirmation on that yet. It would seem, however, that the kidnap victim was not here when the police arrived. And, because of their use of gas, it would seem that the informant tipped them off to that fact when he called. It's a tangled web, but we'll keep you up-to-date on the story as it unfolds. This is Marla Dayle in Queens."

The camera zoomed past her face to focus on the house, where firemen were finishing the work of extinguishing the fire.

David switched off the television.

"Okay, he wasn't there," he said in relief.

"But where is he?" Nicole could know no relief as long as her son was still missing. And it didn't seem that killing the kidnappers was a very good way to go about finding him. "Where is he?"

David had nothing to say in reply.

The telephone rang. Maybe that would be their answer.

Chapter Twelve

"Hello?" David answered the phone with as much authority as he could muster with the thudding pain of anxiety pressing against his heart.

"He's safe," a voice answered. It was Agent Hardin. "We just got word here that your baby is safe and sound."

"You did? Why you?" David demanded. "Why didn't they call here?" Covering the mouthpiece, he whispered to Nicole, "It's Hardin. Someone called about Matt. They claimed he's safe."

Nicole let her breath go at last; it wasn't the news that they wanted, but it was far from the worst they could have had. Still, she was filled with questions that tugged at her heart and made it nearly impossible to wait for a more complete explanation.

"I imagine they know a call to your apartment would be traced immediately," the agent said tiredly. "We weren't expecting the call to come here."

"What did they say? When is he coming back?"

"Soon." The other man paused, thinking either of what to say or of a gentle way to say what he had to tell.

"What did he say?" Nicole asked eagerly at David's shoulder. "Where is Matthew?"

David slipped his arm around her shoulder and held her to him. Her nearness calmed him, keeping him from shouting out in frustration over the phone.

"Look, Mr. Germaine," Hardin said at last, "something is going on with this business that I'm at a loss to explain. The man who called us assured us that there will be no further ransom demands, and that nothing will happen to your son. The police switchboard operator listened to a tape of the call, and she swears that it's the same man who called in the location of the kidnappers."

"Why would he turn them in but not return Matt?"

"That's one of the things we can't figure out. There seems to be no purpose to the man's actions."

"It's quite apparent that Morley Kraft is toying with us," David said, seeing sufficient explanation in the man's obvious cruelty. "He'll make a new demand soon enough."

"Maybe, but there's little point in this. Keeping your son would make sense, but not this way."

"You people sure have a hard time making sense of things down there, don't you?" David snapped. "Probably the best thing either of us can do is get off the line so Kraft can contact me."

"Yes, Mr. Germaine, we had best clear the line." Then he added, "Say, your cabdriver turned out to be a spook."

"A what?"

"Ex-CIA. Dominick Carlotti is his real name. The agency threw him out about five years ago. Other than holding a taxi license, there's very little record of what he's been doing since then. He has spent a considerable amount of time in Australia, however."

"So he might be working for Kraft."

"Maybe."

"Why was he fired from the CIA?"

"The records are sealed," Hardin said. "I have no way of finding out in any reasonable length of time."

"Do you think he has Matthew?" David asked. If so, there might be hope after all. He didn't know the man, of course, but he had gotten the impression that he had a kind heart and that he could be trusted.

"It's possible. Maybe you should listen to the recording, Mr. Germaine. You might recognize the voice."

"I can be there in ten minutes," David offered.

"I meant in the morning," Hardin said. "Whether it is or is not Carlotti makes very little difference at this point."

"I don't care. I'll be right down. Goodbye."

David hung up the phone, feeling as though a light had just begun to glow at the end of the tunnel. He turned to Nicole and tried to explain everything in a rush.

"The guy driving my cab today was fired from the CIA five years ago, for unknown reasons. He's spent time in Australia since then," he said. "I'm assuming that he's working for Kraft in some capacity, though that still doesn't explain why he helped me find the kidnappers this afternoon.''

"Maybe he's playing both ends against the middle,'' Nicole offered. "He could be out for his own gain.''

"Sure, but why didn't he snatch the ransom money, then?''

"There were three of them, David. Maybe he thought the odds were against him.''

"Maybe, but it sounded like they were pretty well in the bag. I don't know for certain, but it sounds as though he picked up Matthew from the kidnappers and then made the call to turn them in right after that. He could probably have overpowered them when he went for Matt, unless...'' He paused, considering what little he knew of the man's possible motives.

"Unless what?''

"Well, it's a stretch, I suppose, but Carlotti struck me as a man with a great fondness for children. We talked quite a bit while we were watching the building this afternoon. Now, I suppose he might have been making it up as he went along, but it sure didn't seem that way. He spoke of his family and how he would deal with anyone who harmed his kids. He was very sincere-sounding.''

"You figure he would have let the money go, just to be certain he got Matt away safely.''

"Right. It's a hunch—and I suppose I'm being overly optimistic—but I think that's why he didn't take the money. He figured that if he started anything, Matt might be injured.''

"Or, more realistically, Mr. Kraft had him do it this way just to double-cross the kidnappers. He surely wouldn't want them alive to testify against him."

"Right, there is always that possibility, too," David admitted. "I just hope I'm right about Carlotti. If I am, that means that Kraft doesn't have Matthew, and we've still got room to maneuver with him."

"You don't want to maneuver, David," Nicole insisted then. "You want him arrested. You want everyone involved with kidnapping our son, including your friend Carlotti, behind bars for the rest of their lives."

"Of course, but it will take an awful lot of luck to accomplish that, Nicole. And I don't see any way to do it, other than retrieving the satellite for him so he can be caught with the goods."

"You can't do that," Nicole said as she paced nervously between the couch and his desk. "He'll throw you overboard as soon as he has what he wants."

"I would assume so," David agreed.

"No, we've got to trap him here, in New York, somehow. If we could just think of some way to get him here, we might be able to do it."

"Awfully hard, since he's not about to come out of the woodwork long enough to be seen anywhere near this mess." David pondered the question a moment. "I just wish I knew where Dominick Carlotti fits into all of this, and whether or not he has Matt now."

Nicole could see no way for them to have any effect on matters, nothing that they could do to bring their boy back to them or to force the rogue millionaire to expose himself to capture. No. Maybe there was one way. Just maybe.

"I think I know how to get Morley Kraft into New York," Nicole said then, sudden inspiration giving her sudden hope. "Do you have his telephone number? Anywhere you can reach him?"

"I have his office in Australia," David said. "Why?"

"I'm going to make a little call," she replied. "But we've got to set the stage a bit first."

As Nicole explained her idea, David began to share her hope. Maybe they could not only get their son back, but also catch Kraft red-handed and provide definite proof of his guilt to the authorities.

If the plan went well, they would be home free. If not, they could all end up dead. That was a chance they'd have to take.

DOMINICK CARLOTTI parked his car on the street before a modest frame house on Long Island and got out. He walked around to the curb and opened the rear door and leaned in to unfasten Matthew's straps and remove him from the child seat.

Matt was fast asleep, his small lips puckering with his breath as his head lolled against his shoulder in repose. Dominick smiled, looking at him. "Cute little guy, aren't you?" he whispered. "Hate to wake you, but it's no good sleeping in a car seat, anyway. Let's get you inside."

He had unclasped the safety straps and was about to take the child out of the car when the sound of movement behind him caught his attention. He began to pull his head out of the car, but was stopped by a sudden blow to his back, just above his right hip. His knees buckled, and he flailed at the door for balance as he fell out of the car. Another blow rolled him over, a brief view of his attacker's face flashing past his disoriented eyes. Then he was kicked viciously in the side of the head, and the world became black around him.

Garth Donnelly stood over Dominick for a moment, waiting for any movement. When the man remained still, he leaned into the car and took the still-slumbering child from his seat. Carrying him carefully—he didn't want the brat to wake up and give them away with crying—he crossed the street and opened the door of a battered Ford.

He had the bottom half of a cardboard orange box strapped into the passenger seat with the seat belt, and he laid Matt into that to keep him in place. The child barely fit, lying in a fetal position. Matt stirred a bit uncomfortably, but didn't wake up. He'd had a big day already.

Garth got behind the wheel and started the car and then drove away carefully, though the rusted muffler didn't allow for a quiet exit.

"Now we'll see who's playing the game," the Australian said. "And I'll show them who's best at winning."

WHEN NICOLE AND DAVID left the precinct house, it was nearly one in the morning, but the streets were still alive with activity as they walked down the broad concrete steps to the sidewalk and stood for a moment before the building.

The taped voice had indeed been that of Dominick Carlotti, the ex-CIA agent who had been David's cabdriver that afternoon. Knowing that didn't make them feel any better, however. Neither did the kind tone of the man's voice when he assured the police that Matt was all right and that nothing would happen to him. No matter who had their son, or what his intentions might be, Matthew was still missing. And, even were he to be returned this moment, Morley Kraft was still waiting for David to provide the key to regaining his fortune.

Compounding their problem was new evidence the police had obtained about the kidnappers.

The two children David had taken from the day-care had themselves been kidnapped from their home in Connecticut a week earlier. A demand for five hundred thousand dollars in ransom had been made, with a drop-off in Central Park, just like the one Nicole and David had been instructed to do for Matthew. The payment was to have been made the previous night, but it had been called off at the last moment, for some reason.

"It looks like they saw a chance at a bigger haul and postponed this one," Agent Harkin said. "They were professional kidnappers, and there is some evidence that they were involved in the illegal adoption racket, too."

The police didn't believe the Australian had anything to do with the kidnapping. They'd decided that it was a simple kidnapping for ransom, undertaken by a gang who made their living doing exactly that.

Of course, the authorities weren't giving up on finding Matthew. No, with the identification of Carlotti as the man on the phone, they seemed to think they had a greater chance of finding him than before. But that was as far as they would be going. As far as removing the threat posed by Morley Kraft was concerned, Nicole and David were on their own.

In front of the police station, Nicole walked quickly away from David without looking back. He paused a moment, then followed, trotting to catch up with her.

"Come on, Nicole, you can understand my position, can't you?" he asked her plaintively. "I can't give in."

"I'm only interested in the safety of my child," she shot back angrily. "Surely you can deal with this person, David. The police don't believe you. Can't you get that through your head?"

She stopped then, facing him to make her point.

"They think you're a paranoid fool, and frankly, I'm beginning to think the same thing. If you would have handled this business from the start, we wouldn't be in this mess now. Our son wouldn't be in this mess! But no, you had to stand on some kind of principle, didn't you? While you're looking for the moral high ground, people are suffering in the real world. Now get back into the real world and give the man what he wants."

"No, I can't," David insisted, leaving it go at that.

"Then you can find someplace else to sleep tonight," she replied.

"It's my apartment, too," he pleaded.

"Yes, but though you obviously don't care, my son is missing, and I need to be near the phone. Good night, David!"

She stalked away, leaving her husband standing openmouthed and dejected, clearly at a loss to defend his position in the argument, and equally unable to change it.

Nicole turned the corner, crossing the street to where she hoped to catch a cab for home. As she did, she had the unmistakable impression of eyes on her. Malicious eyes, watching her walk away with calculation and cunning. An image of Garth Donnelly flashed through her mind, and he looked so real she could almost have sworn he was standing there on the street behind her.

But that couldn't be. He was dead—or, if not dead, he was surely lying low in Mexico someplace, recuperating from his injuries. He wasn't in New York City.

Nicole hadn't thought of the man since the sinking of the *Katharine*. At the time, he had been a threat, and she hadn't thought of consequences when she fired the flare pistol at his departing speedboat. Since then, she hadn't had time to ponder her actions and contemplate the very real possibility that she might have caused a man's death.

Though it was certainly possible that he had survived, the police didn't think so. After all, they'd found his boat, but no sign of him. Nobody could swim that far to shore against the tide. In her heart,

Nicole had believed him dead, too. She pushed that thought aside, not wanting to dwell on it.

In truth, she rather hoped he wasn't dead, for she'd hate to live with the thought of having caused anyone's death, but she had to admit that it would be better for all if the villainous man were dead. She'd be safer, and it would certainly be easier to get their son back without his interference.

As she walked, the impression of being watched faded, but the memory remained in her mind, haunting her with doubt. What if he was alive and here in New York? She'd just separated herself from David, giving the evil man the perfect opportunity to...

Stop that, Nicole, you're scaring yourself. He isn't here. You've got to be strong, if you're going to get Matthew back. You simply have got to be strong.

When a taxi stopped for her, she felt better. He wasn't there at all. Of course, she had hoped that someone would be watching them, so that their plan could work. She just didn't want it to be Garth Donnelly.

DAVID TOOK a separate taxi to Jerry Brunsvold's apartment and rang the bell, feeling nervous about the whole thing. It could very easily go wrong, terribly wrong, and he was out of touch with her and unable to do anything about it. It didn't seem like a very good plan, when it demanded that they lose contact with each other. They had to rely on other people behaving in a predictable manner, and only fools bet on predictability.

Jerry eventually answered his ringing with a groggy "Yes?" over the intercom.

"It's me, David. Let me in."

The door lock buzzed, and David walked into the building and pressed the button for the elevator. Some strange sensation made him turn and look around him just then, but there was nothing out of the ordinary in the foyer of the apartment building.

It was strange, though. For a moment he'd had a feeling of someone following him. Nothing more than a notion, really, yet the feeling went with him up the elevator to Jerry's floor.

"What are you doing?"

Jerry opened the door dressed in his pajamas, with a robe thrown hastily over them. He regarded David with a mixture of anxiety and annoyance as he waited for an explanation.

"I've got to make it look as if she's thrown me out," he told his partner. He walked quickly across to the living room window and looked out and then drew the blinds.

"Thrown you out?" Jerry rubbed his eyes sleepily, yawning. "I'm having difficulty following you, David. Most people who are thrown out of their homes want to conceal that fact."

"She hasn't, really, you jerk." David crossed to Jerry's kitchen. "Do you have any food here?" Neither man had expected to be back for several months, and so neither was very well stocked with groceries at the moment.

"Canned soup," Jerry said. "I've got lots of canned soup. They keep putting it on sale, and I keep buying it, but I never eat it. So what's the deal with Nicole?"

"Well, we figure someone is watching us for Kraft. Maybe not all the time, but some of it, anyway. So we had a little tiff outside the police station, and Nicole went to the apartment alone," David explained while he searched through Jerry's cupboards. "She's going to call Kraft and tell him she wants to make a deal for Matthew. She's going to tell him that the reason they didn't find the satellite at the coordinates Ben gave them was because I'd already recovered it."

"You? Why would you do that and not give it back to the government? This plan sounds a bit shaky," Jerry commented.

"I want the chip for myself. It's a guidance and tracking program, right?" David said. "Well, she'll tell him that I planned to rework the design a bit to use in a remote submarine probe. Then I'll patent the whole thing as my own original work and make a bundle off of royalties on it. She'll say I tried to give it to the feds, but they didn't care."

"But, while you're willing to turn a personal profit, you aren't willing to turn it over to a weapons dealer," Jerry concluded for him.

"Of course not," David said, fussing with Jerry's coffeemaker. "I'm morally repulsed by the very thought of that."

"How does this help anything?" Jerry asked, watching him pour water in the machine and turn it on.

"She knows where the satellite is, and she wants to hand it over to Kraft in exchange for Matt. But she won't deal with any middleman, only Kraft himself. She doesn't trust anyone else to keep their word. See?"

"What a horrible plan," Jerry moaned.

"I'll be sure to tell Nicole what you said about her plan," David told him.

"Her plan?" Jerry yawned and then smiled. "Well, if Nicole thought of it, it might work after all."

"And if I had, it wouldn't?"

"Not likely." Jerry laughed. "Well, at least you've got a bug on your phone line, so the police can keep up with you on this mess."

"She's not going to use our phone," David said. He found a can of tuna and pondered it while he talked. "She'll call from the pay phone at the entrance to my building, and ask that Kraft call her back at that line."

"What? David, you're nuts! Both of you!"

"Come on, Jerry, Kraft has a big business going for him. Most of his money comes from weapons and security systems. Don't you think he routinely scans calls for electronic listening devices? He'd be on to us in a flash."

"But you told the FBI, right?"

"Hell, no. They couldn't find their way out of a paper bag," David said. "Don't worry, we'll let them in on the finale. We just don't want them botching things in the preliminary phase."

"Why all the secrecy? I have no doubt you'll get Matt back. He doesn't want to keep him, David. And he doesn't want the money."

"No, but he wants the satellite," David said evenly. "And he won't leave us alone until he has it. We won't be safe unless we catch him in the act of handing our son back to us. We've got to get something against him that will stick."

NICOLE HELD the slip of paper on which she'd written Morley Kraft's number tightly in one hand and left the apartment with great determination. She might have trouble selling Kraft on the idea that David would have recovered the satellite for his own gain, but she hoped his own ruthless nature would allow him to believe that anyone was capable of such behavior. It was a stretch, of course, to believe that anyone would allow his child's life to be placed in jeopardy for the sake of monetary gain, but that was exactly what she had to convince him that David was doing.

Deep in her heart, she didn't believe Matthew was in any real danger. Kraft needed him healthy as a sign of good faith, after all. But she didn't expect that any of them would remain healthy for very long once the millionaire had what he wanted. Witnesses were a distinct liability in criminal undertakings.

Nicole's heart was pounding as she took the elevator down to the small foyer of the building. To think that a couple of days ago she'd been tucked away on the campus of a small college, ready to take her final exams. So much had happened since then that she could barely keep track of it all.

The best thing that had happened was that she'd gotten her husband back. Nothing could compare with their reunion, and it seemed that they would be able to smooth over the rough patches brought on by their separation.

She'd been foolish to leave, she could see that now. Foolish and selfish and unwilling to give him a chance to accept the idea of a child. He had been foolish, too, to ever have made such general statements about children. She supposed now that it was fairly natural for men to be clods about such things. She would have to give him some leeway in areas like that.

She smiled tightly as the elevator door opened onto the lobby and she stepped out. A small room with a couch and two chairs served as an entrance to the building, where people could wait for the occupants to come down. It was tastefully decorated in pastel colors, but the furniture was a bit frayed after years of use. Mailboxes filled one of the walls, while the others were unadorned.

A pay phone hung on the wall opposite the elevator, and Nicole walked quickly over and picked up the receiver. She wanted to get this over with before she lost her nerve.

Using her long-distance calling card, she dialed and waited for a response.

"Kraft Company, Morley Kraft's office, may I help you?" said a businesslike receptionist.

"Is Mr. Kraft in?" Nicole didn't expect that he would be, of course.

"I am sorry, but Mr. Kraft is out of the country on business at the moment," the woman said. "May I take a message?"

"Yes, you may." Nicole spoke with even determination. "My name is Nicole Ellis Germaine, and I must speak to Mr. Kraft immediately."

"Nicole Ellis Germaine," the woman repeated. "Can you tell me the nature of your business with Mr. Kraft?"

"It's personal business," she said. "He should know exactly what it is when you tell him. I want him to call me back at this number in exactly one hour."

"One hour? Well, I don't know if he can be reached . . ."

"Reach him," Nicole said. "Tell him if he doesn't call in one hour, all bets are off." Nicole gave her the number of the pay phone in the foyer, and then repeated it for good measure. "Are we clear on this now?"

"Yes, I believe so," the receptionist said. "What time is it in New York now?" she asked.

"Two a.m. on the nose," Nicole said. "Why?"

"I want everything straight, is all," she said. "I shall try to relay your message to Mr. Kraft, Mrs. Germaine."

"You do that," Nicole said. Then she hung up.

A feeling of giddy fear swept over Nicole almost immediately after hanging up the telephone. Her palms became moist, and a clammy chill seeped through her body.

She'd done this much, anyway!

But maybe the worst was yet to come.

DOMINICK CARLOTTI had staggered into his house and managed to make it through to the bathroom just in time to throw up. His head hurt horribly, and his vision wavered and doubled with every movement. Still, vomiting made him feel a bit better.

"Dominick, what are you doing?"

Lucille Carlotti, his wife of twenty-one years, was outside the bathroom when he emerged. He had said he would be bringing home a surprise when he came, so she had waited up.

"Are you all right?" she asked him. Then she saw the purple, swelling bruise behind his left ear, and rushed forward to examine it with a gasp. "What have you been up to?"

"No good, dear," he said, trying to smile. He walked to the couch in the living room and fell back onto it, resting his head against the wall tiredly. There was no way on earth that he could explain how he could lose a baby. Not even he could understand his lack of readiness for an attack, and he didn't want to worry her unduly with such details. And, if his still-fuzzy memory was correct—if that *had* been Garth Donnelly standing over him on the grass beyond his house—then things were looking darker than he had hoped. He surely didn't dare tell that to Lucille.

"You know that you should never have gotten hooked up with that Kraft again, don't you," Lucille said, perching on the arm of the couch and looking down at her husband with worried reproach. "It's not going to help you one bit with the agency."

"I don't care about the agency anymore," he said. "But I can't go out the way I did. I've got to clear it up."

"No one accused you of doing anything illegal," she said. "Why can't you let it go?"

"Because I can't," he said. "Not now, especially. Boy, when I went back with Kraft last year, I never expected to hit something as big as all of this. Lucy, I've got him by the tail now. All I need is for a couple of things to go my way, and he's dead meat."

"Or you are," she advised him. She stroked his graying hair, looking tenderly down at the determined pug of a face she'd loved since she first set eyes on it. "We need Papa around the house, you know. The kids need you. And Mama gets lonely, too."

"In a few days, it will be through, one way or another," he said. "I promise." He held her hand and looked into her eyes with the look that meant, *I love you, but let's not talk about it anymore.*

He didn't say how he'd gotten the lump on the head, and she knew better than to ask. Fifteen years as a CIA wife had taught her the value of not asking. When he was discharged, disgraced in the field and all but accused of letting a foreign agent escape, she had seen it as a good thing. Now they could lead normal lives. But, for Dominick, there would be no normal life until his name was cleared. Even though only a handful of people would know the difference, Dominick couldn't let it go.

Maybe now he would finally be free of his obsession.

Over an hour later, Dominick received a telephone call from Morley Kraft that sent him out the door once more. Before he left, he checked the .38 caliber revolver he'd been wearing beneath his jacket. Even more alarming to Lucille was the fact that he loaded his big gun, too—a .357 Magnum—and left the house with both weapons.

Now she wished she had asked more about what was happening. Now she wished she had found a way to stop him.

IT WAS nearly three o'clock. Nicole had been pacing the apartment for most of the time since calling Kraft's office in Sydney. She'd gone over her story again and again, and she wished David were there to rehearse it with.

One thing about the earlier call had troubled her. Why had the woman wanted to know the time in New York? Sydney time should be all that mattered to her. Was there something important in that question?

Nicole managed to sit for five minutes, her nervous tension flowing out through her fingers in doodles on a pad. "Why ask New York time?" she wrote, and circled it several times. Underlined and circled and boxed in with ink. And then she was up and pacing again until the clock finally agreed to let her get it over with.

She left the apartment praying that he would call, and believe her, and agree to meet her. It seemed like far too long a list to ask for. As she took the elevator down again, she felt that the plan was bound to fail. How could she possibly be lucky enough to have everything go right at one time.

The elevator stopped, and the doors opened. Nicole took a deep breath and stepped out, staring at the telephone on the wall before her. *Here goes, I hope.*

She didn't notice the man leaning against the wall by the elevator until he moved. It was too late by then, of course, for the barrel of a gun was pressed roughly into the small of her back as a large hand clasped her shoulder from behind.

"Well, well . . ." said the well-remembered Australian voice. "Here's our little flare shooter, come out to play. I don't even have to go up, do I?"

The telephone rang.

"Donnelly, I can't . . . Please!" she cried out.

"Of course you can, missy." He marched her past the phone and out the front door. "It's time for the mother-and-child reunion."

Behind her, the telephone continued to ring.

Chapter Thirteen

David burst into the apartment with Jerry close behind him at nearly four o'clock in the morning. "Nicole!" he called out, but there was no reply. "Nicole!" Nothing, and all the rooms of the apartment were empty.

He had waited as patiently as possible for Nicole to call with word on their plan, but the telephone had remained stubbornly silent. He'd picked up the receiver several times to be certain that it was working at all, and it always was. He almost wished it was broken.

Now he stood in the living room, looking around in puzzled fear, as he wondered what could possibly have gone wrong.

"No sign of a struggle," Jerry said. He slipped his hands in his pockets and stood immobile, watching David as he looked around the room in confusion.

"Damn," David said. "If someone abducted her, why isn't there some sign of it? And, if not, why didn't she call? Where is she?"

"Maybe Kraft decided that returning her call was too impersonal," Jerry offered. "He sent someone to meet her face-to-face."

"You don't think he could have found out what phone the number was for?"

"Sure he could," Jerry said. "He's got the reach to find out anything."

"I'd better call the police," David said as he walked to the telephone.

"Wait," Jerry said, hurrying to stop him. "Maybe you should wait and see if you hear from him. You might not want to involve them yet."

"Hey, a couple of hours ago you were advising me to get the cops in on our plan. Now you say not to? Why the change of heart?"

"It just seems that since you've started this without official sanction, you might as well let it play awhile longer. Like when we were running soundings off the Azores, looking for that downed cargo jet? We ran the robot sub past the crash site, and we were going to pull it up and start on a new grid, but we didn't. We let her run, and found the plane."

"This is hardly the same thing."

"No, but it has a similar feeling," Jerry said. "Just leave them out of it for now. They won't be able to do anything but wait, anyway. There's no evidence to get them started here."

"You're right about that," David admitted. "Nicole wouldn't have let anyone into the apartment of her own free will, and if they forced their way in, there'd be signs of a struggle. But there's nothing."

"Would she have gone to meet them without you?"

"No. We were going to set her up with one of the small homing devices we used for our dolphin survey, and she was going to sew the minirecorder into her sweater. She wasn't wearing the recorder or the homing device yet."

"And you needed both for the plan to work," Jerry said, thoughtfully. "So we know she didn't go to meet them. Maybe she's at the market. I don't suppose you've got any more food than I do."

"We picked up a few provisions on the way home earlier."

"You're not leaving us much room for hope, are you?"

"No," David said glumly, "I don't see much hope, either." He collapsed into the chair by the telephone and stared at it, wondering if he should call Kraft's number and offer to get it done with.

"Boy, not much more over an hour into the plan, and it's already gone haywire," Jerry commented, taking a seat on the couch facing David.

"This is not an especially good time to say 'I told you so,' Jerry."

"No, I . . . Well, I suppose it does seem that way," the scientist admitted. "But it's not what I meant. What I mean is that it seems as though a random variable has been introduced into the plan. Something foreign."

"Well, yes, I do admit it seems a bit strange that Kraft would do something against Nicole. Especially so fast. What do we have to go by? She's gone, with no sign of a struggle," David said, starting to tick off his points on his fingers as he spoke. "She didn't call us with any news about Kraft's return call, which would seem to indicate that she didn't receive one. There is no benefit to Morley Kraft in kidnapping Nicole—especially if he spoke to her and heard her offer. And he couldn't have arranged to snatch her fast enough for her to have talked to him and yet not called us about it.''

''In other words,'' Jerry said, nodding his agreement with David's conclusion. ''She was probably abducted outside the apartment, either on her way up from making the first call or down to wait for the return call.''

''That would be my guess, yes. So, who would do it?'' David asked. ''There's no benefit to Kraft. Carlotti? I can't see any reason there, either. Of course, I can't see any reason for his actions at all. He's certainly a random variable.''

''Not really so random. He comes into this thing from a definite angle, David, and he seems to be benign. You're right about him, of course, for he doesn't seem to have anything to gain from taking Nicole.''

''But who does, and why? Nobody.''

David sighed, pushing his hair back with both hands and thinking how he had planned to get a real haircut once they got to the mainland. Now he found he couldn't even touch his hair without thinking about his wife and wondering if she was all right.

Having calmed somewhat since entering the apartment, David was able to look around him with a less frantic view of things. Was there anything out of place, anything changed that might help? No, nothing about the physical space was different from the way it had been earlier. But there was writing on the notepad by the telephone. That much was different.

"Here, look at this," he said, picking up the pad.

"Why ask New York time?" Jerry read from the pad.

"That's a lot of question marks," David said. "So it was a big question for her."

"How do you know?"

"Nicole doodles when she's thinking," he explained. "And she reinforces big questions just like that. I can't think of what she meant by that, unless—sure, whomever she spoke to in Sydney probably asked what time it was when Nicole called."

"Meaning what? It seems like a normal question," Jerry said.

"Yes, it does," David admitted. He couldn't think of why she would have concerned herself with an innocuous question from a secretary halfway around the world.

"Well, at least we know that she did make the first call," Jerry said. "But we're not getting any closer to finding out what happened to her."

"Wait a minute! Why did she ask the time?" David stared at the pad in his hand.

"Why should a secretary in Sydney worry about the time in New York? Nicole was going to give Morley an hour to return her call. If he was in Sydney, then Sydney time was all he had to worry about. New York time wouldn't matter—unless he was already in New York! Sure, that's it! And if he's here already, he could well have had her taken before he knew about her call to him."

"But why?"

"That doesn't matter," David said excitedly. "We've got to check customs at the airport to see if he entered the country legally. And we'll need to find out if there have been any arrivals of Kraftco airplanes in the last twenty-four hours or so that he might have slipped in on. And there's the land border, too. Do you know anyone who can get us information about passports?"

"That's quite a pile of work to do in an awfully short time."

"You're right, we'll never figure it out this way." David was up and pacing now, talking with nervous energy. "He wouldn't want to enter the country, anyway. There's too many creditors who want to talk to him for him to just stroll on into the country. If I were him, I'd be keeping as low a profile as possible. Yes, that's it," he said, stopping excitedly in front of Jerry. "Doesn't he have a yacht? Sure, what's the name of that big stinkpot he owns? It's a corporate yacht, I think. I'll bet he's keeping it at sea so the banks can't seize it. *Gambler's Luck*—that's the name of the ship!"

"He's probably sitting outside territorial waters, waiting for this thing to be resolved," Jerry offered. "I still don't think he snatched Nicole, though. Why should he?"

"I don't know, but he's all we've got at the moment. Let's see if we can find that yacht."

NICOLE HADN'T STRUGGLED against the man; it seemed pointless to do so. She allowed him to march her out the door to the battered car at the curb, in a state of confusion.

Why was Kraft calling, if he'd sent this man to kidnap her? What was that crack about her child supposed to mean? Clearly, there was something going on at which she and David could not have guessed. How did the newly resurrected Garth Donnelly fit into everything?

As they reached the car, movement in the front seat caught her attention immediately. It looked like a small head bobbing up from behind the bench of the seat, and the muffled sound of a child's voice came to her from within.

Nicole burst forward instinctively, and Donnelly let her run to the car and around to the passenger door, where Matthew peered through the glass. But the door was locked, and Nicole could only crouch down and smile at her son, standing in the box belted to the seat, and play a kind of pat-a-cake with him through the barrier of the glass.

"Open the car," she demanded of her abductor. "Open it, please."

Donnelly opened the driver's door and stood grinning at her over the top of the car. "There," he said, "that's nice and polite of you. Very nice and polite. I like that."

He slid the keys over the roof of the car to her.

"Open it up," he commanded. "I've got my gun inside, so don't try anything."

Nicole took the key and turned it in the lock of the door, then threw it open to claim her son in a loving embrace. Matthew clung to her neck, burbling a happy hello to his mother.

"Okay, now, little mother," Donnelly said, "why don't you pull that box out of there and sit down with Junior? Mind now, there's no place to run to that I couldn't shoot both of you before you reach it."

Nicole had considered running, thinking she might be able to make it into the trees of the park, at her back. But Central Park wasn't a natural forest, and there was scant undergrowth at the edge to provide immediate cover for a fleeing woman carrying a small child. He was absolutely right about her having no time to find a hiding place before he could shoot her, and she knew he wouldn't hesitate for a moment to kill her.

Holding Matthew on her hip, Nicole reached in and unclasped the buckle of the seat belt and pulled the box out onto the pavement.

"That's right," Donnelly said. "Just leave that there. Some hobo can use it as an apartment." He laughed harshly, then rapped his knuckles on the roof of the car. "Get in."

Nicole did so, buckling herself in and then holding Matt tightly to her as the man slipped behind the wheel and started the car. He placed his gun on his seat, between his legs, and pulled away from the curb, whistling tunelessly.

"We need diapers," Nicole said. She wasn't about to let this man bully her concerning the care of her son. He might hold her against her will, but he could not shut her up on that subject.

"I'll stop at a market," he said flatly.

"And food," she continued. "I don't know how long you're planning to hold us, but a baby needs food and diapers and a warm place to sleep."

"Crying little brat needs a whack in the mouth, is what he needs."

"You touch him and you'll have to deal with me, Donnelly," she said angrily.

"Oh, I'd like to deal with you, missy, yes, I would. I'd deal really nice with you."

Nicole didn't say anything else. The memory of his hands on her at her apartment building flashed through her mind, reminding her to keep her tongue under control. The man was capable of anything— that had already been proved to her.

They had already driven through the city and through the Holland Tunnel into New Jersey. They were in a heavily industrial area. While most of the Garden State was, indeed, as pretty as a garden, this part definitely was not. Nicole wasn't sure where they were; she'd lost track of their movements while taking care of her son.

He seemed to be in good condition. Someone had changed his diaper, and judging from the stains on his brand-new outfit, they had fed him as well. It was obvious that he needed changing now, however. If he didn't get the wet diaper removed quickly, he'd become cranky, and that might upset their captor.

"He's wet," she said after a while.

"Yeah, I can smell him." Donnelly laughed.

"Here's an all-night market." She pointed at the illuminated sign passing on their right. "Why didn't you stop there?"

"Too close to the city, and too big."

"Well, you've got to stop soon, or he'll get a rash. You don't want him crying."

"No, we don't want Little Lord Fancy Pants to get a red bum, do we? Relax, missy, I'll stop for your diapers."

It was clear from the sureness with which he drove that he knew his way around the area quite well. They made several turns, taking them through darkened neighborhoods and past factories either shut down for the night or running under the bright illumination of yard lights.

"Your boss is being a fool," she said after a few minutes. "I was going to make a deal with him. That's why I called him."

"Oh, you did, did you? What kind of a deal could you have made with Kraft?"

"Well, that hardly matters now, does it? He's kidnapped both me and my child, and I'm not about to make any deals."

"That's fine," Donnelly said. "Kidnapping is a foolish crime, and only fools commit it."

"Fools like you?"

"Yeah, like me." He laughed again, seeming to find a great deal of humor in the idea of his own foolishness. "Here's someplace we can get diapers."

He parked the car in front of the broad glass window of the store. From this position, he could see most of the counter inside.

"You better have money," Nicole said. "I'm not about to pay for the pleasure of being kidnapped by you."

Looking at the counter, she could see where he would be able to see her standing there, but he wouldn't be able to see her hands. She might be able to do something to call attention to her plight while she was inside.

"Okay," he said, handing her a twenty-dollar bill. "You buy your diapers and food and whatever you can get for twenty. I'll sit here with the kid and watch. You understand what will happen if you try anything funny?"

"I understand." She didn't think he would actually harm Matthew, but he might well drive away with him and leave her behind, childless again.

Nicole passed Matt to the man with dread, and then, after chucking her son under the chin, she opened the door and got out. A minute later she was inside and crossing to the aisle marked Baby Supplies.

A tired-looking young woman behind the counter watched her enter, but apparently satisfied that she wasn't going to steal anything, she went back to her crossword puzzle. Nicole picked out diapers and then collected applesauce and a couple of frozen "junior dinners" designed for a child of Matthew's age, while trying to think of some way to get word of her location out to David. There was no way that she could think of.

Then she saw the credit card scanner on the checkout stand. If she paid with her plastic instead of Donnelly's cash, it would register where the purchase had been made.

But would it be quick enough? She didn't know, but she knew she had to try. Hurrying now, she removed the card from her purse while the shelves of the store concealed her from Donnelly's watchful eye, then carried her purchases to the counter with the card folded into the bill he'd given her.

The clerk rang up the items. "Twenty-four ninety-seven," she said.

Nicole handed her the card. While she was busy verifying the account, Nicole made as much of a show as possible of opening her purse and removing her billfold and taking money out. Then, lowering her hands to where she knew they would be out of sight, she slipped the money—and Donnelly's twenty—back into the billfold. She slipped the credit card inside, too, once the clerk was done with it.

"There you go," the clerk said. "Have a good day now."

"You too," Nicole said, halfheartedly wondering if her ploy had been to no avail.

She left the store quickly and returned to the car where she put the bag of groceries into the back seat and resumed her place in front with Donnelly and her son.

"You owe me $4.97," she said.

"Bill me."

Donnelly put the car in gear and pulled away from the store, taking them out into the brightening light of dawn, just as the world was beginning to rise for work once more.

"THERE HASN'T BEEN any ransom demand," David said. "Nothing for an hour."

"I haven't been able to trace Kraft's ship, either," Jerry said.

He had returned to his own apartment to make the calls required in his effort to find Kraft's yacht. He had just returned, hoping for good news from David to brighten his own mood, but had been disappointed. Both men sat staring wordlessly at each other for a moment.

"Marine phone connections," Jerry said after a minute. "God, David, I forgot about Able Davis. Remember him? Drunken bum from college? He's with Satcom now, some kind of administrative position. He could probably get us a record of any call made from Sydney to the yacht. That would tell us where the ship is!"

"Can you call him now?" David asked.

"Almost four? Hell, I don't know how he'd like a call at this time in the morning," Jerry said. "I haven't seen him in a couple of years, at least. But there's no sense in waiting, is there? I've got his number here someplace."

Jerry took his wallet out and began rummaging through a collection of business cards and notes he'd written to remind himself of things he'd subsequently forgotten. There was no money in the wallet; he kept that in a pants pocket.

"I know one other thing we can do, too." David smiled, nodding as he took his own wallet out and removed one of his credit cards. "It's a long shot, but maybe if I cancel the credit card Nicole is carrying, they'll show a purchase on their alert list.''

"Major long shot," Jerry said, still looking for the number. "I don't know if you should cancel it, though. What if she gets away and needs it for cash?"

"That would be another major long shot," David said. "As much as I hate to admit it, I don't think she'll be getting away from these people until we arrange her release."

He dialed the number on the back of his credit card and punched in answers to the voice-mail questions that answered his call. Finally he got a human operator.

"Hi, I need to cancel my card," he said. "Well, no, it's more than that, actually. What I'm hoping to do is to find out if any purchases are made on it in the next couple days."

"You don't want to cancel it?" the operator asked suspiciously. "But you want to know if it is used?"

"Yes, that's right. I can find that out, can't I? It is my card."

"Oh, yes, sir, you can certainly be advised of usage. We'll send you an itemized list with your next bill."

"No, that won't do. I'll need to find out over the phone," he said, quickly. "If I were to call in a couple hours, I'd want someone to be able to tell me. Can that be done?"

"I suppose so...but, well, wait a second and I'll ask my supervisor how to handle that."

The woman left the phone, and David cupped his hand over the mouthpiece and turned to Jerry. "They want to send me a list at the end of the month," he told him.

"Sir, could you give me your card number?" She took the number down, repeating it after David read it to her. "And when would you like this trace to begin?"

"Right away," he said. "No, how about an hour ago? That would be even better."

"Just a moment, sir." The operator left the line again.

"An hour ago?" Jerry snorted. "Sure, some guy snatched her, and then Nicole sprang for pizza on the way out of town."

"Sir, we do have a charge on that account," the woman said.

"Really? When?"

"Only about ten minutes ago. The card was used at an Auto Express in Newark, New Jersey. The charge was for twenty-four dollars and ninety-seven cents."

"God, that's great! Is there any other information?"

"No, sir, that Auto Express isn't equipped with our charge link, so I can't tell you what they purchased until we receive the statement."

"That's perfect. Wonderful! Thank you!"

David hung up the phone, feeling as if someone had just given him a Christmas present. He beamed at Jerry, who had finally found the phone number in his wallet.

"She charged twenty-four dollars and ninety-seven cents at Auto Express in Newark, New Jersey." David bolted out of his chair and grabbed his jacket. "Can you man the phone in case they call?"

"Where are you going?"

"I'm going to New Jersey!"

And with that, David was out the door.

"HELLO, I need to make a credit-card call."

Nicole spoke as quietly as she could into the receiver while watching the door of the motel room warily. Donnelly had gone out, leaving her handcuffed to the frame of the bed. He hadn't checked whether she could reach the phone or her purse, however, and she had been able to extract her phone card and reach the telephone to dial. She had hoped to speed things up by dialing the operator, rather than risk misdialing the long series of numbers needed for a credit card call.

"You can dial your number direct, ma'am," the man on the line said.

"Yes, I know, but I'm in a hurry. Please, it's an emergency."

She watched the door, her stomach churning at the thought that it might open at any moment. He had said mysteriously that he was going to check things out and would be back "shortly." How long a period of time that might represent, she wasn't sure, but she knew it wouldn't be much.

Fortunately, Matthew had dropped off to sleep once she'd changed and fed him. He was a wonderfully adaptable boy, much like his father in his ability to take things in stride. She hoped that she was showing even a modicum of his talent for rolling with the punches.

"What number are you calling, please?" the operator asked.

Nicole gave him David's number and then the number of the card. Then she waited for what seemed to be hours while the phone rang at the other end.

Please, please be there! Don't be at Jerry's, because I don't remember that number! And don't you dare be out looking for me, David! Be there by the phone! Be there!

"Hello?"

It was Jerry!

"Jerry, it's me! Nicole! I'm in—"

But she was cut off by Garth Donnelly's hand depressing the switch on the base of the phone, as another hand calmly snatched the receiver from her fingers and slammed it against the side of her head.

"Okay," Donnelly said as he stood over her. "Here's where we teach you how to mind your manners."

Nicole could do nothing but cower against the bed and wait for the man's cruel lesson to begin.

Chapter Fourteen

"Hello? Hello, Nicole? Hello!"

Jerry shouted into the phone frantically and stabbed his finger against the switch, hoping for some miracle to restore the connection. It was no use—they had been cut off.

But the line was tapped. She'd known that when she called! All he had to do was contact the police to find out where the call had originated from.

Jerry looked around the table for the number the FBI technicians had left when they completed the connection of their tracing equipment. He couldn't see it anywhere. Desperate now, he searched a wider area, hoping to find the number until he finally found it on the table in the kitchen. Taking the paper with him, he ran back to the phone and dialed.

"Hello, FBI?" Jerry was nearly incoherent by the time someone answered. He wasn't used to events happening at such a rate of speed. His temperament was better suited to the measured pace of scientific events, not the rush of intrigue.

"Oh, you want Agent Charles," a man answered. "Just a second."

The second was more like five minutes, and Jerry pulled the phone off the table so that he could pace the room while he waited.

"Yes," came a voice finally.

"Did you get that call? This is Jerry Brunsvold. I'm at David Germaine's apartment. We just got a call from Nicole. Did you get the source of the call?"

"Source? Wait a second. Why would you be interested in calls coming from the wife?"

"She's missing!" he exclaimed. "Oh, never mind, just tell me, did you trace it?"

"Must have. It just came in, you say? I was out of the room, but the equipment is on. Sure, I've got the number. It'll take a couple minutes to get the location for the number. Are you still at the apartment?"

"Yes, I said I was, didn't I?"

"Fine. Just calm down and wait. I'll call you back with the location." The agent hung up.

Jerry replaced the receiver and began pacing again. *God, if this keeps up I'm going to develop an ulcer.*

DAVID PULLED into the parking lot of the Auto Express in Newark, New Jersey, at five-thirty in the morning, and ran inside.

"Hey, have you been on duty all night?" he asked the woman behind the counter.

She regarded him skeptically, obviously wondering whether the wild-eyed man before her was dangerous or not. She shrugged, deciding that he might be crazy but wasn't dangerous.

"Sure," she said. "Since eleven last night. Eleven to seven."

"Great. I'm wondering about someone who made a purchase an hour or so ago. Someone who paid with a credit card. Do you remember anything about them?"

"Paid with plastic?" She yawned and rubbed at her shoulder as she looked blankly at David. "Yes, I guess I can remember that much in a night. Not many customers at night."

"What about this one?"

"Why do you want to know? And how do I know that I should tell you anything about her?"

"It was a woman? Sandy hair and hazel eyes? About this tall?" he asked, holding his hand up just above his shoulder.

"Yes, about that." She nodded, saying nothing more.

"She paid $24.97 for something," David said in exasperation. "What was it? Did she give any indication where she was going?"

"Well, I suppose if you know how much she paid, you must be legit enough," the clerk said. "She bought diapers and some junior meals. Oh, and applesauce."

"Diapers?" David whooped out the word, laughing. "She bought diapers? Oh, God, thank you! Oh, wonderful!"

He could have kissed the woman, if she hadn't backed away from his outburst. Instead, he drummed the tips of his fingers on the countertop in excitement.

"Do you remember anything else about her? Please, anything."

"Well, she came in a dirty old Ford. Gray, I think, or else it was just that dirty. There was a man with a kid waiting in the car."

"Do you remember anything about the man?"

"No, he was tall and the sun visor was down."

"What about where they were going? Any idea?"

"No. They drove south from here. Came from the north and left to the south. I know that because the muffler on the car was shot, so I looked up when they came in, and I had nothing better to do than watch them leave."

"This is wonderful," David exclaimed. "Nearly wonderful, anyway. You don't know how much you've helped me tonight. Here, buy yourself something nice."

He dropped a twenty-dollar bill on the counter and walked to the door.

"Twenty bucks? Boy, you really are happy she bought diapers, aren't you?"

"You'll never know how happy," he said as he walked out the door.

He stopped at the pay phone outside the door of the store and dialed his home number to share the news with Jerry. The line was busy. Maybe there'd be good news when he did get through. Maybe they'd already found her.

David decided to wait a couple minutes and then call again, while he tried to think of some place that Nicole might have been taken.

If I were a kidnapper, where would I hide a woman and child?

He had no idea, but he was heartened by the fact that Nicole and Matthew were together. Everything was bound to work out for the best now.

"HERE'S WHAT HAPPENS to little girls who disobey!"

Garth Donnelly pulled Nicole's free hand back from her face, jerking her arm up over the bed so that she was pulled nearly onto the bed before the cuff on her other wrist stopped her. He grasped her blouse and tore it open, buttons flying and clattering against the walls and floor like BBs.

Nicole tried to stifle her cry of alarm. She didn't want to wake Matthew—not for something like this! No, and as much as she wanted to call attention to her plight, she didn't dare scream out, for fear of the beating she might receive to silence her. She was at the man's mercy, and he was a man who knew no mercy.

Donnelly grabbed her bra in his broad fist and lifted her by it, pulling until the garment snapped and dropped her back to the floor beside the bed. When she tried to cover herself, he slapped her and then pulled her leg out so that she was on her back on the motel floor, exposed and vulnerable to his assault.

Nicole gritted her teeth as he knelt and touched her breasts, squeezing them roughly in his hands as he grinned down at her. She fought back tears as his hands moved down to her jeans and unzipped them so that the pink silk of her underwear was visible to his prying eyes.

He touched her stomach with both hands and slid them up over her breasts to her throat, then grasped her jaw in one hand and squeezed her cheeks in until she could taste blood.

"Is this what you want?" he asked. "Should I rape you for good measure, missy? Tell me! Should I do that?" He slapped her, still holding her jaw in one hand. "Should I do that?"

"No," she whispered, barely able to talk past the fear that gripped her.

"No, what?" He released her mouth, but stayed kneeling beside her, his eyes piercing her with laser intensity.

"No, please don't do that," she said. Tears welled up and flowed from her eyes. "Please, please, oh, God, please!"

"All right. I only wanted you to ask politely." He stood, grinning with pleasure at having made her beg. "I'm not a rapist," he said.

Nicole pushed herself back to the bed until she could sit up and clutch her torn blouse over her breasts. Tears flowed unabated to wet the garment in her hand.

"Remember that, little missy." Donnelly lit a cigarette and leaned against the bedside table as he looked at her. "I probably won't rape you, but I'll sure as hell kill you if you give me any more trouble. I'll kill you and sell your kid overseas. They pay top dollar for blond babies. Blond boys are in high demand everywhere."

"Please don't," she said, feeling totally broken.

"You behave yourself, and you'll be fine," he said.

Nicole looked up at the man, seeing him for the monster he was and knowing that he meant every word that he said. But she felt some of her spirit returning to her as she regarded the smirking man. She had to regain some of her humanity and self-respect in some way.

"That was inhuman," she said quietly, as though afraid to talk. "What you did was inhuman."

"I've sunk low enough to get involved with kidnapping," he said. "I suppose scaring a woman isn't any lower than that."

"You know what I mean. You enjoy making me suffer, don't you?"

"If I really wanted you to suffer, I'd have finished what you thought I was starting. I could make you suffer if I wanted that. I figure I owed you as much as you got, anyway."

"Why? Why do I owe you anything?"

"For this, you bitch!" He pulled at his own shirt, the snaps popping open and revealing a layer of stained gauze covering his chest. "Hell of a burn you gave me with your popgun. It hurts like the blazes."

"You killed Ben Tucker," she said. The sight of the many stains his oozing burns had created in the gauze wrapping sickened her, but it made her glad in a way, too. This man deserved to suffer.

"Ben Tucker is free from suffering now, though, isn't he?" He drew deeply on his cigarette, letting the smoke curl out of his nose as he snapped his shirt again. "You talk about suffering. Dear Ben Tucker isn't suffering. And I promise that you won't be suffering if you cross me, either. Dead people can't suffer.''

He laughed and coughed a bit on his cigarette. Then he stubbed the butt out and knelt to unlock her cuff.

"We're leaving," he said. "Get your ass in gear."

Nicole hastened to comply obediently. Soon, though, very soon, she'd find a way to become the master of the situation. Soon this monster would be obeying his victim's commands.

"HELLO?" Jerry snatched up the telephone on the first ring, eager to hear where Nicole had called from, only to be disappointed by the fact that it was his friend Able Davis calling him back. "Oh, hello. Did you find anything?"

"Sure, buddy, though it isn't exactly legal me telling you," the man said. "I figure any time a straight arrow such as yourself asks someone to break the rules for him, there must be a good reason."

"Yes, and I'll fill you in someday, Able," Jerry said. "I've got to clear the line soon, though, so I don't have the time now."

"No sweat. The call from Sydney to the *Gambler's Luck* came right here. Almost, anyway. The ship is off the coast of New Jersey."

"You're sure of that?"

"Gotta be sure, or the satellite can't make the connection. He's off the coast, all right. In fact, he made a call into the city at three this morning, but nobody answered."

"Great. I owe you a big one, Able," Jerry said. "I'll get back to you in a couple days."

"You can pay me back by never waking me in the middle of the night again," the other man said. "Take care now."

He hung up, and Jerry did the same, wondering if the FBI had already tried to call, and if he should call them.

The phone rang, and he pounced on it.

"Hello? Jerry, it's me," David said. "I'm at the Auto Express where the card was used. It was Nicole! She bought diapers!"

"What? I don't think I heard you right," Jerry said. "Did you say that she bought diapers?"

"Yes, diapers. She's with Matt! See? She's with Matthew!"

"Oh, sure, great! I didn't understand. That's wonderful."

"I can't tell where they went from here," David was saying already. "I'm hoping you've got some news."

"Yes, but I won't have all of it until the FBI calls me back," Jerry explained. "Nicole called, David. She said hello, and I think she was about to tell me where she was when she was cut off. The feds are matching the number with an address now."

"She called? We'll have her soon, Jerry. Listen, I'm at a pay phone. I'll call back in five minutes. Is that long enough for them to contact you?"

"It should be. Hang up so they can get through. I told you to get call waiting on your line, David. You're too damn cheap for your own good."

"Right. I'll hang up. This feels good, Jerry. I think we're getting close. Bye."

Jerry hung up, feeling none of his partner's enthusiasm. David hadn't heard the frantic tone of Nicole's voice, after all. He hadn't heard her panic, and he would have known how desperate the situation was if he had. Nicole didn't panic easily, but she'd definitely been scared on the phone.

Jerry didn't see where Nicole and Matthew being together was really very good news at all. It merely made it all the easier to lose both of them at once.

When the phone rang this time, Jerry answered, half fearing it would be a telemarketer selling time-shares in condos, but it was finally the FBI.

"We've got the trace for you," the man said. "But we're unclear about the circumstances of the call. What does Mrs. Germaine have to do with incoming calls? She should be there with you."

"She's not," Jerry said. "We don't know where she is, but we will if you'll tell me where the call came from. Her husband is waiting to hear."

"It came from the Garden Villa Motel in Newark, New Jersey," he said. "That's on the New Jersey Turnpike, just southwest of here."

"Garden Villa," Jerry repeated as he wrote the information down on the pad. "Thank you very much."

"Wait a second, Agent Hardin wants to talk to you."

"I don't have time to—"

"Brunsvold? This is Hardin." The other agent got on the line, sounding angry. "What the hell is going on? How did you people manage to lose Mrs. Germaine?"

"It's pretty easy, really," Jerry said. "But I don't have time to tell you. David is going to call back for that location in about one minute. I've got to hang up."

"What in hell is he doing?" Agent Hardin roared.

"He's in New Jersey," Jerry said, adding, "Oh, you might be interested in knowing that Morley Kraft is sitting on a yacht just off the Jersey coast right now. Pretty coincidental, if he doesn't have anything to do with the kidnapping, isn't it? Maybe you guys should do a bit more checking on David's explanation before passing him off as paranoid."

"How do you know where Kraft is?"

"No time now, Agent. Goodbye."

Jerry hung up the phone and then lifted the receiver briefly to make sure the connection was broken to clear the way for David's call.

The phone rang not more than thirty seconds later.

BUT WHILE DAVID was talking to Jerry, his son was being carried out of a nondescript motel by a tall blond man, while Nicole followed carrying a grocery bag clutched tightly to her chest. They got into the battered gray Ford and drove away to disappear into the morning traffic on the freeway.

They were nothing more than another car among the many cars now. They were hidden as well as the fabled needle in a haystack, and this time they were headed north and east, back into New York City.

Chapter Fifteen

Morley Kraft was standing on the sand, looking at the surf pounding the Jersey shore. His hands were hidden in the pockets of the trousers of his Armani suit. The jacket was buttoned against the wind that had come up since the helicopter had brought him in, just skimming the tops of the waves.

As he waited, a car pulled off the road and parked farther up the beach. Dominick Carlotti got out of the car and ran toward him.

"Who snatched the kid?" Dominick asked. "I had him with me, and somebody clubbed me from behind and took him."

Dominick was pretty certain now that it had been Donnelly, but he wanted to see the other man's reaction to the question. Morley didn't disappoint him; his gaze narrowed slightly as he thought, and then his eyes widened with incomprehension.

"Why on earth would I have the child taken from you, Dominick? Come now, your years with the CIA have left you jaded. I don't want the baby. I want the chip in the satellite. Now, what I am wondering is, who might have taken the lovely Ms. Germaine away from us just as she was going to make a deal? Would you possibly know that?''

Dominick was confused now. He didn't know Kraft terribly well, but he did know that whenever he spoke in such a deliberate manner, it meant that he was using extra words to buy time for thought. He was clearly disturbed and confused by something; maybe he really didn't know about the child.

"I don't know anything about Nicole Germaine," Dominick said. "But my bet is on Donnelly."

"Garth? He's dead, Dom. He drowned off California. Drowned or burned, or something." Kraft dismissed the issue with a wave of one hand. "No, not Donnelly."

"That's who clubbed me," Dominick said. "That's who took the baby."

"Then why did you— Oh." Kraft smiled. "So, did I pass your little lie-detector test, Dominick? Do you trust me now?"

"I've never trusted you. But I believe you don't know about the kid. So, what's the deal with Donnelly? Why would he want to double-cross you?"

"Money, of course," Kraft said, as they began to walk to Dominick's car. "There are other people after that satellite, you know. They have made him many offers."

"And he just now decided to turn against you?"

Dominick knew there had to be something more than that to prompt such a loyal servant as Garth Donnelly to suddenly go into business for himself.

"There may be a bit of anger involved, too," Kraft admitted. "I sent his dossier to the U.S. authorities after the boat incident. It's not an entirely truthful document, you realize, but it does contain some key facts about his rather shady career. Part of it might even help to clear up your troubles with your agency."

"I don't imagine you did me any favors, Kraft. So you figure that Donnelly found out that you turned him over to the feds to avoid having Germaine's story find a believer?"

"Exactly. I covered my ass." Kraft smiled. "At the expense of Donnelly's. Of course, I believed him dead."

"But you'd have done it anyway," Dominick said.

"Yes, certainly. I hate loose ends." Arriving at the car, Kraft leaned against the top and looked across at Dominick as he opened his door. "Incidentally, I thank you for taking care of my loose ends with those day-care people."

"You wanted me to watch Germaine." Dominick shrugged. "You should thank the cops."

"I'll make a nice donation to the Policemen's Benevolent Fund." Kraft opened his door and got in.

Dominick paused for a moment, thinking of his options. If he killed Morley Kraft right now and left him lying on the beach, with the murder weapon lying at the bottom of the Atlantic, the chances were good that he could get away with it. It would solve at least half of Germaine's problems, and get Kraft out of his way while he went after Donnelly. It was Garth Donnelly he wanted, after all. He was Dominick's Southeast Asia contact, after all, not Kraft. It was

Donnelly who had let three North Korean agents go free, and made it look as if it were his ineptitude that had allowed their escape.

Maybe he should just kill Kraft and be done with him.

No, there was no point crossing over to their side of the equation. The tape recorder in his jacket had certainly picked up enough evidence against the millionaire to help both himself and Germaine. The man had all but hanged himself already. No, he would stick to his plan and allow circumstances to tighten the noose.

Dominick got into the car and drove them off of the beach and back to civilization.

THE GARDEN VILLA MOTEL was an ugly L-shaped structure that had seen better days. David pushed the bell under the sign that told him to Ring Bell for Manager and waited impatiently until an elderly man in a robe came to the door to scowl at him. He wasn't eager to make any statements about the guests, but fifty dollars convinced him to check his scruples for a moment or two and tell David that a couple with a small boy had checked into unit eleven.

"But they're gone now," he called to David's back as he began to hurry down the row of doors to number eleven.

"What? How can you be sure of that?"

"Damn busted muffler woke me," the man complained. "I heard them coming and going. There ought to be a law against noise pollution."

"There is," David said, with a feeling of dismay clutching at his heart. Kraft's man had caught her making the call, and had been smart enough to know the line would be tapped. He'd moved them before they could be found. "Can I take a look in number eleven?"

"Look ahead." The man disappeared inside for a moment, reappearing again with a key. "Just drop the key through the slot when you're done. I'm tired of getting up for nothing."

"WHERE ARE WE GOING?"

The sunlight stung Nicole's eyes, and the visor meant to shade her was missing on the passenger side of the old car. Matthew fussed in her arms, tugging at a frayed bit of cloth where a button had torn free from her blouse.

"We're going to make a call and arrange to trade you in for something of value." Donnelly spoke brusquely, looking tired and in pain. "Do you have any suggestions where to make the deal? It's in your best interests that you pick a place that I can tell your husband about without letting the cops know. Your phone line is tapped, you know."

"Yes, I understand." She looked out of the window, watching the cars on the highway and the factories along the road on which they were all traveling. "The deli," she said, with little thought. "Tell him the deli, and he'll know exactly where you mean."

"And where is this deli?"

"Downtown. Manhattan. It won't be too busy at, say, ten o'clock. We can meet him there. I know he'll come alone."

"Oh, I know he will, too. That was a pretty nice little bit of drama you two played out last night in front of the cop house." The man laughed, squinting against the sun as he drove.

"You were watching," she said.

"Yes. I thought you saw me for a minute."

"I felt you there," she said. "Like an animal lurking in the tall grass."

"I like that one," he said, laughing. "An animal in the tall grass. What, a lion?"

"A skunk," she replied.

She looked away from him while he laughed. He wasn't an easy man to insult.

"Right then, the deli it is," Donnelly said. "Let's call your better half, eh? Tell him his battered half is ready to come home."

Nicole had figured out that Morley Kraft knew nothing about Donnelly's actions. He couldn't know, otherwise Donnelly would have had his plan worked out already. He wouldn't be making it up on the fly. That meant there was no organization backing Donnelly up, no one to help him pull the whole thing off. If she could just break away for a moment in the mid-morning crowd. If she could cry "Rape!" or "Murder!" or anything else that focused eyes on the blond monster, she might have a chance. All Donnelly had was her.

And that was the problem. All he had was her, and so he would be desperate not to lose her. More than that, he had her, and she had Matt. She dared not risk her son's life.

There was nothing she could do but wait and take what opportunity might come her way.

JERRY BRUNSVOLD was asleep in the chair beside the telephone when it rang. He jolted awake, disoriented at first. He grabbed the receiver on the third ring.

"Hello?"

"The deli," a man said. "Ten o'clock. Come alone, and bring the location with you. The real coordinates this time. Mama is waiting."

"Hello? Wait! Hold on a second!" But it was no use—the man had hung up.

Still half fogged from sleep, Jerry scrambled to find a pen and write the message down before he could forget it. Glancing at his watch, he added that the call had come in at 8:30. Now, if David would get back, perhaps he could shed some light on what the message meant.

The telephone rang again.

"Hello, this is Hardin," the man said, before Jerry could say hello. "Germaine?"

"It's Jerry Brunsvold," the scientist said then. He stood and stretched, fighting against the kink a night in the chair had put in his back.

"Where's Germaine? What are you people up to?"

"Did you check into Kraft any further?" Jerry asked. He wasn't about to answer any questions until he got some answers of his own. "He's on his yacht right now."

"His yacht is missing at the moment," the agent said. Apparently he had decided to play by Jerry's rules, without further intervention. "It filed a travel plan for the Virgin Islands and passed through the Panama Canal a week ago, but it never got to the islands. There's been no word since then.''

''He's trying to keep it away from the banks, isn't he?''

''That's what we figure. But that's pretty normal for a man in his financial condition. It's not actually illegal.''

''Have you got anything on his connection to Garth Donnelly?''

''He's not connected. After Donnelly drowned in California, Australia sent us a dossier on him. He's strictly free-lance. There was a connection to Dominick Carlotti, though,'' the agent told him. ''It looks like Donnelly was in the spy business as one of Carlotti's contacts. Apparently he crossed Carlotti up on something and framed him for it. He went underground after that.''

''So that's why Carlotti is messed up in it.''

''No, he was working for Kraft four years ago. He quit and moved back to New York and took that taxi job. We think he's back on Kraft's payroll now, but that doesn't prove anything. If Kraft was really mixed up in this, as you insist, he wouldn't have sent Carlotti to work against his own plan.''

''Unless Carlotti is clean and he's working on his own plan.''

''Mr. Brunsvold, you've got to face the fact that a millionaire with Morley Kraft's visibility can't afford to be mixed up in kidnapping and extortion.''

"What color is the sky where you live, Hardin?" Jerry asked. He'd heard that line on television once, and had always wanted to use it on someone.

"Where's Germaine?" Hardin sounded tired of playing games with Jerry.

"I don't know. You can bet I'll have him call you when he gets back, Agent."

"Goodbye."

Jerry hung up feeling frazzled. He needed more sleep than he had gotten. Staying true to form, however, he wrote the new information Hardin had given him on another sheet from the pad and slipped it into his shirt pocket with the first.

Now for some coffee.

The door was flung open before he got halfway to the kitchen, and David rushed in.

"Any news?" he asked quickly. David looked as though he had run back from New Jersey, his cheeks flushed and hair blown askew.

"You've had a couple calls," Jerry began, but the telephone interrupted him. "I'd better get that," he said. "It might be Hardin again."

David ran to the den and picked up that receiver as Jerry answered in the living room.

"Germaine there?" It was Dominick Carlotti!

"I'm here!" David shouted in reply. "What is going on? What are you trying to do to me?"

"Stop jabbering and listen," the man said. "Kraft is with me. Where do you want him?"

"What?" David's view of things was twisted again, another plot unfolding within the several plots he already knew about. "Why do you have Kraft?"

Jerry was in the den then, tugging at his sleeve like a child trying to get his parent's attention. He thrust two sheets of paper into David's hand and stepped back.

"You want Kraft, don't you?" Dominick asked as David read the papers. "Just tell me where to bring him."

"The deli," David said. "Ten o'clock."

"What deli? Come on, Germaine, I haven't got a lot of time."

"Hoffman's Deli. Downtown."

"Hoffman's? Hey, I know that place. My old man used to take us there, years ago. Must be fifteen years since I've been in the joint."

"Well, be there at ten this morning. I don't know what's going on. I thought I was already supposed to meet Kraft there."

"Why would you think that?"

"He called. Or someone called for him. They've got Nicole and Matthew and want to trade them for information."

"He doesn't have them," Dominick said. "You say you're meeting them at ten at the deli?"

"Yes. But who am I meeting?"

"Garth Donnelly," Dominick said seriously. "You'd better bring a gun, Mr. Germaine. I may not be able to cover you this time."

Dominick hung up before David could ask any further questions, and he replaced his own receiver with icy fingers.

Donnelly was alive! He was alive, and he had Nicole!

"YOU AREN'T really planning to let us live, are you?"

Nicole was tired from sitting in the car so long. Matthew was heavy in her lap, cutting off the circulation to her feet, even with all of his squirming. She wanted it all to be over more than anything else in the world.

"I don't need to kill you," the man said. "I'm going to fade away and never be seen again once I get the numbers from your old man."

"Sure, and my check is in the mail," she said scornfully. "You're going to kill all of us."

"In broad daylight? Give me some credit," he snapped. "Look, I've got a buyer for the satellite. All they want is the location, and they'll take the rest from there. All I want is fifteen million American dollars in cash. That's plenty to get away on."

"But where? Where can you go that they won't find you?"

"You're living in a fantasy world, if you really believe the law is so all-powerful that I can't get away from them. They're bloody fools. Most of them are bureaucrats with mounds of paper filling their desks. They won't find me, dear. And I won't kill you."

"Thank God for small favors," Nicole said.

Donnelly laughed.

"It's twenty to ten," he said. "Shall we stop for a bite at the deli?"

Chapter Sixteen

Marion Hoffman was standing behind the counter in the deli, slicing pastrami, when the three new customers walked in. She didn't look up at first, but continued running the slicer, her eyes firmly on the whirring blade. When she finished what she felt was enough for the noon rush, she wrapped the remainder of the meat and put it away and covered the bin of sliced pastrami behind the glass front of the counter.

Then she looked up at the newcomers.

A tall blond man had approached the counter and was looking at the selections behind the glass, while holding the hand of a woman behind him, who was busy looking around the deli as though searching for something. Marion couldn't see her face, but something about her hair, the way she carried herself, made Marion feel as though she knew her from someplace.

But this woman was carrying a child. She didn't know anybody outside of her own granddaughter, Amelia, who would be that age and with a baby.

"Can I help you?" Marion asked the man.

"Yeah, I'll take pastrami on rye," he said. He had a Bronx accent, but it sounded like an acquired accent—as if he were a foreigner who'd lived in the city for ten years or so and blended his original accent with a new one.

"The lady wants an onion bagel with cream cheese. A plain bagel for the kid, with lots of cream cheese," he said then. "Isn't that right, honey?"

He turned to the woman for approval, and when she looked back at him, Marion's heart seemed to stop in her chest.

She did know her! She had dreamed about this woman! My God, she was here!

Marion turned and looked at the calendar without thinking about the action. It was still May, not September 6.

The woman was dressed in jeans and wearing a white blouse that was tied above her navel, rather than buttoned, and she was not wearing a bra. That wasn't how she had been dressed in Marion's dream. In fact, as nice a day as it was, it wasn't really fitting attire for the current weather.

The man she was with was totally unfamiliar to Marion. Tall, blond, he was wearing a long, dark coat and Dockers. His coat was held shut by one button at the waist. He appeared calm, much calmer than the woman who accompanied him.

No, Marion hadn't dreamed of either the man or the baby. But this woman was definitely part of her dreaming, and the feeling of danger that seemed to waft from the man before her was very similar to the feeling she'd gotten from the small man in sunglasses of whom she had dreamed.

Marion looked at the clock. It was 9:55. The time was wrong, too.

"Yes," the woman said then. "Onion bagel with cream cheese would be fine. I don't know if Matt will like cream cheese, but we'll give it a try."

When the woman spoke, Marion's perception of her shifted again. Now she was familiar for another reason. She had worked in the area, and had been in two or three times a week for lunch.

"Excuse me," Marion said. She looked closely at Nicole, noticing that she was wearing her makeup awfully thick for such a young person. Her face seemed a bit puffy, too. "Don't you work in the neighborhood? Work for some lawyer, maybe?"

"Yes, Clint Forrester, but he died. I haven't lived in town for over three years."

"I didn't think I'd seen you in a while." Marion began filling their order as she spoke, her fright fading as she began to find a reason for recognizing the woman, if not for putting her into her dreams. "So how has life been treating you lately? God's granted you a child, I see. You weren't married when you were working for the lawyer, were you?"

"No, I got married shortly after his death." Nicole was trying to be friendly, but her heart wasn't in it. Any minute, her husband would be there. "Matthew is fourteen months old."

"Matthew, is it? Such a good, strong name."

Marion Hoffman placed their order on the counter and rang up the charge and then leaned to chuck the little boy under the chin while the man in the dark coat paid for the meal. He was a happy little boy, so sweet, but she noticed that his parents didn't wash him very well.

Looking up at Nicole from this lower angle, she noticed the dark bruise beneath her chin. It looked like someone had choked her. And the makeup... From this angle, it looked dark and mottled. The pool girl had been beaten! That was why she wore her makeup so thick!

Marion straightened up, trying to think of something to say, some way to offer help to this poor woman, but they took their food and backed away.

"Thank you," Nicole said. Matthew waved and giggled in her arms.

Marion watched them take a table in the corner between the windows overlooking the two intersecting streets. She wanted to call the police and report that brute. Could she do that? Would they do anything if she did?

"She noticed your bruises," Garth said as they sat. "You didn't do a very good job with the makeup."

"I was in a moving car," Nicole said. "Besides, you shouldn't have hit me."

"My, you're getting feisty now that Papa is getting closer, aren't you?" He unbuttoned his coat and opened it so that she could see the butt of the boxy black gun hung on a string around his neck beneath it. "Don't get too feisty, little missy," he said. "I'm ready for that."

Nicole would have said something in reply, but the room suddenly seemed to jump around her. There was the sound of glass breaking, and when she looked up, she saw that the front window had shattered. There was blood everywhere!

And then the vision was gone. Nothing had happened. Nothing at all. But Nicole was left with the cold certainty that it would happen.

It would happen very soon.

DOMINICK CARLOTTI parked the car in a pay ramp a block away from the deli, and he and Morley Kraft began walking to the rendezvous. It was nearly ten. They were going to be a couple of minutes late.

Kraft walked with his hands in the pockets of the overcoat he'd put on. In his right hand, he held the .357 Magnum that Dominick had brought from home. Dominick had insisted that he have some kind of protection, but Kraft didn't like the idea. He wasn't sure he wanted to be anywhere near a place where such protection might be deemed necessary.

Dominick was glad he'd managed to convince him to take the gun. The serial numbers had been filed off it, so if he used it or was caught with it, the millionaire would be guilty of a weapons violation, as well as his other crimes. Dominick wanted to be absolutely certain with this guy.

Of course, if everything went well, Garth Donnelly would kill him. That would be a pleasant turn of events indeed. Just as long as nobody killed Donnelly, Dominick would be happy.

"Germaine is really going to give me the numbers?" Kraft asked again. For a self-made millionaire, he seemed awfully unsure of himself.

"He'll do anything to get his wife and kid back," Dominick said.

"But we don't have them."

"He doesn't know that, does he?" Dominick laughed, thinking of how much *Kraft* didn't know. He'd learn fast, all right. Very soon.

DAVID TOOK A TAXI to the deli, trying to formulate some kind of plan for when he got there. He couldn't think of anything. All he could do was to give the man the numbers he carried in his pocket and hope he would fade into the crowd without a fuss.

The thought of dealing with Garth Donnelly made him shiver, a clammy sweat coating his brow. Nicole and Matt would be there. They would be in the line of fire if anything happened.

Nicole and Matthew would be there, and that was the only thought that guided his actions now. It was the only thing that mattered.

Besides, when Dominick called his apartment, he had been speaking on a tapped line. The FBI had been listening, and that was a fact of which he must have been aware. The feds would be here, too, somewhere. They would be waiting to capture Donnelly once he'd released Nicole and Matthew.

His cab stopped before the deli at a minute before ten, by David's watch. He paid the fare and got out, feeling as though he had a target hung around his neck. He took a deep breath and stepped up to the door of the deli.

There have been gunshots on this doorstep before, he thought. *Nicole died here once before.*

Pushing that horrid thought aside, he opened the door and walked inside.

A young couple—lawyers or accountants, from the look of them—were at a table near the counter, with papers spread out before them. The gray-haired woman at the counter was standing very still and staring at him as though she had seen a ghost. A man sat alone by the side window, sipping coffee and reading the sports pages.

And there they were, at the corner table. Nicole was in the very corner, with Matthew in her lap. Garth Donnelly, looking remarkably healthy for a dead man, was seated at her side, with his back against the wall and both hands hidden beneath the table. He nodded toward David. Nicole smiled. There were plates on the table before them, and Donnelly had obviously just finished a sandwich.

David turned fully toward them and slowly slipped his hand into the pocket of his jacket. He could see Donnelly grow tense at this action, but he did nothing more. David withdrew the paper with the coordinates for the satellite on it and held it out slightly, with a shrug of defeat.

Donnelly smiled and brought one hand up to motion for David to approach the table. He did so, feeling as though he were moving through five feet of water.

They looked healthy. Matthew was smiling and doing his best to eat a bagel, with cream cheese smeared all over his face. Nicole looked pensive, but none the worse for wear. A bagel with cream cheese sat untouched on the table before her. Only when he got to the table was David able to see that she was wearing makeup. A great deal of makeup. And she was wearing her blouse oddly. It appeared to be tied like a beach bum's shirt, but he couldn't be certain, looking past the bulk of Matthew in her lap.

What was wrong? Nicole never wore makeup.

Her face was swollen! He had beaten her and torn her blouse! What else had he done to her?

David's hands clenched at his sides, and he almost gave in to the urge to lunge at the man beside his wife and beat him senseless. He had beaten his dear Nicole!

Nicole saw his tension, however, and shook her head. *No, don't be my knight in shining armor just now. Not when we're so close to getting free of him!*

He sat, his back to the restaurant.

"You've got the numbers?" Donnelly spoke quietly.

David didn't say anything at first; he couldn't trust himself to speak yet.

"Hear this?" Donnelly said. There was a double clicking sound. "I just put my weapon on automatic. Try anything, and you'll be in the center of one of those mass-murder things you Americans love so well."

"I understand," David said.

"Right, then, do you have the correct numbers?"

"Right here." David put the paper on the table between them. He was through holding out or caring what anyone did with the information that he was handing over to the man. All he wanted to do was to get his wife and child back safely.

"Very good," Donnelly said, taking the paper and slipping it in the breast pocket of his shirt, beneath the long coat. "Have a bagel while you're here," he suggested. "Your wife doesn't seem to have much of an appetite."

"I'm not very hungry, either."

David watched Nicole, taking note of the nervous movements of her eyes and trying to gauge the degree of the swelling that was nearly concealed by her makeup. It angered him anew to look at her. What had this man done to her?

"Are we through with this?" David asked. "Can we leave?"

"Why the rush, mate? Is there someone waiting outside for me? Maybe I should use the back door?"

"I haven't told anyone about this meeting. And I don't care what door you use, as long as you use it quickly."

"I will," Donnelly said. "There's nothing to keep me here, you can believe that. I'll leave you to tell old Morley Kraft whatever you wish about the merchandise."

"I'll be happy to give him the numbers, too, should he request them," David said. "I don't really care anymore."

"That would have been a good attitude to have had from the start, mate. You could have made some money on this deal."

"This is pointless." David stood up. "Come on, Nicole, let's get out of here."

Nicole saw him stand as a thrumming sound filled her head. It was as though the air had come alive and were talking to her, warning her to stay seated, to stay down and keep Matthew down. David was looking at her oddly, a pleading look in his eyes, but she couldn't hear what he was saying past the throbbing in her ears. Her own body seemed to be screaming at her, *Stay down!*

The door of the shop opened, and both David and Garth Donnelly turned to look at the same time. A tall, balding man in an overcoat had entered, accompanied by a shorter, pug-faced man in a leather bomber jacket. The short man stepped away from the taller, obviously putting distance between them.

And Garth Donnelly stood, flipping his coat back as he reached for the weapon hanging from a length of twine around his neck. He shouted something, making the tall newcomer flinch and jam one hand into his pocket.

Nicole shouted, too, grabbing the ceramic plate holding her bagel and throwing it at the back of Donnelly's head. Then she pulled at his coat, distracting him just long enough to allow the other man to bring his hand out of his pocket with a gun in it.

David dived at Donnelly then, hitting him in the shoulder just as he fired a burst from the automatic weapon in his hand. The bullets struck the far wall, just over the tall man's head.

He twisted away from David, leaping to the side across the restaurant, and kicking a table over to duck down and fire again as the bald man stood in the center of the window, trying to get a clear shot at Donnelly.

The long burst from the automatic weapon knocked the other man back through the window that was already exploding behind him. Glass flew everywhere as people both inside and outside the deli screamed and ran for cover.

''Donnelly!'' The short man yelled and fired as Donnelly turned toward him.

The bullet struck Donnelly in the stomach, knocking him back against the service counter, but he brought his weapon up and fired, and the other man fell behind the table where the two people in suits had been sitting a moment earlier.

Inexplicably, David yelled out then and charged at Donnelly. The evil Australian fired again, but only one shot rang out this time. His weapon was empty.

But, in horrible slow motion, Nicole saw her husband stop his foward motion, his body jerking to a halt as the single bullet tore out of his back and through his left shoulder, and struck the wall over Nicole's head. David staggered, then continued toward Donnelly, who was already slamming another clip of ammunition into his weapon.

And then Nicole saw Marion Hoffman rise up behind the counter with the huge cleaver in her hand.

Marion Hoffman was a gentle woman who had never committed a violent act in her life. She'd never even spanked her children. But she grabbed the first weapon at hand now and stood with anger running like ice water in her veins. This was not going to happen in her shop!

She swung the cleaver with both hands, closing her eyes even as she did, and she struck something that trembled at the blow. Then the cleaver was wrenched from her grasp, and she heard a man screaming.

She couldn't open her eyes. No, she just didn't want to see what she had done. But there was no more gun-fire. And only one man was crying out in pain.

Then someone shouted, "Everybody stop it! This is the FBI! Hands up, Donnelly!"

Marion opened her eyes and was shocked by the sight of seven men with drawn guns standing outside her shattered front window and aiming their weapons directly at her!

WHEN THE CLEAVER struck Donnelly's shoulder, his arm went immediately limp, and he was unable to hold the gun. He fell to his knees, the cleaver still lodged against the shoulder bone, and screamed in pain.

David grabbed his weapon and pulled it free, snapping the twine that held it, and Donnelly fell to his back on the floor made slick by his blood.

Now, faced with a platoon of FBI agents aiming their guns at him, David threw the automatic weapon aside quickly.

"Don't shoot Donnelly!" Dominick Carlotti staggered out from behind the toppled table, shouting at the agents. "Don't kill him now!"

David paid no further attention to the other people in the room. No, it was only his wife and son that interested him, and they were running to him as the room began to waver before him as he sat heavily in a chair.

"Oh, God, David!" Nicole cried out as she embraced him. "Oh, I love you so much!"

Her husband fainted in her arms, slumping against the table, weak from loss of blood from the bullet wound. But she knew she wouldn't lose him now. They'd survived her nightmare, and would emerge to be a family again.

She just knew that they would make it, just as surely as she knew she was finally done dreaming.

Epilogue

Marion Hoffman carried a platter of sandwiches over to the big table in front of the new front window of the shop with a big smile on her face. The Germaines were like family to her now; their son, Matthew, had the run of the shop whenever they stopped in. And her family had taken to them as quickly as she had, forming a bond of friendship that seemed to have a predetermined quality to it.

Their friend, Dominick Carlotti, was a different matter of course. She remembered him from when he was a youngster coming in with his father. The scamp had always tried to steal hard-boiled eggs from the counter before they gave up and put them behind the glass. It didn't appear that he had changed much in the intervening years, except that he was working for the government, which, she supposed, made his thieving ways legal.

She put the platter down on the table now, happy to serve them now that they were no longer being followed by a crowd of reporters and government legal flunkies.

What a hubbub there had been when David first got out of the hospital! And all during Garth Donnelly's trial! Goodness, the deli had been so crowded with news reporters looking for a story that there was hardly room for her regular customers.

With the conviction of Donnelly, and Carlotti's reinstatement at the CIA—though they were still very vague about what Donnelly had originally done to get him thrown out—things had begun to cool down. Now Marion and her family finally had time to take a break during the day, and, after months of nonstop money-making business, it was nice to be able to say that business was slow.

"Sit down, Marion," Nicole said, trying to get Matthew to keep his bib on. "Rest a bit."

"No, the potato salad won't wait," she protested. "You eat, eat! You're much too thin."

"Well, she won't be for long," David exclaimed. "Next February, Marion, we'll be bringing our little daughter around to see you!"

"You're expecting! Oh, my stars, that's wonderful. A girl? But how do you know?"

"We've had the test," Nicole said. "I'm tired of surprises."

"A little girl." Wonderful, just wonderful. "Do you have a name for her yet?"

"Yes," Nicole said. "We're planning to name her Marion Jordan Germaine. If you don't mind, that is."

"Mind? Oh, how could I mind such a thing? Marion Jordan... Oh, I don't know what to say."

The older woman couldn't say anything, really. She was too choked by emotion to utter a word. Matthew filled in the gap, however. He slapped his hands on the table and shouted, "Gramma Marion!" at the top of his lungs.

Marion held her apron to her face and beamed at the little boy, while everyone at the table burst out laughing. Such a group of people, she thought. It was more than a dream come true to have such people in her life.

Had Nicole been able to read her thoughts, she would have agreed. Looking at her husband now as he wiped mustard from Matthew's cheek, she couldn't believe there had ever been a time when they'd been apart. She could not imagine their ever being apart again, either.

No, they would never be apart again. Not in this lifetime.

Are you a word sleuth? If so, find the hidden clues and help Lyssa Carlyle and Craig Rival recover a stolen heirloom claimed by both their families—a diamond wedding necklace passed from groom to bride in
SOMETHING BORROWED, SOMETHING BLUE by Adrianne Lee!
(Harlequin Intrigue #296, coming next month)

S	B	E	D	A	N	I	C	C	O	A	D	T	A
L	Q	U	A	S	Y	X	B	R	N	O	E	R	N
E	D	M	A	U	R	D	M	C	A	X	E	L	A
W	L	E	G	S	M	N	Q	O	E	I	R	Y	M
E	S	O	S	P	S	E	U	M	N	V	G	S	E
J	U	C	R	I	E	S	H	Z	G	T	E	T	T
D	S	B	O	C	R	P	E	N	E	R	A	A	A
E	P	R	U	I	E	E	I	L	R	A	A	E	N
W	E	I	B	O	E	D	R	A	E	Y	C	O	O
O	N	D	L	N	D	R	L	I	T	C	T	V	M
R	S	E	O	E	Y	K	O	L	A	D	I	B	S
R	E	C	W	U	W	V	O	M	R	P	I	R	S
O	D	C	Z	F	L	A	M	H	B	A	C	K	P
B	L	U	E	M	O	R	F	G	D	U	E	F	P

CLUES:

LYSSA	DESIRE	CRAIG
GREED	HEIRLOOM	SUSPENSE
WEDDING	SUSPICION	BORROWED JEWELS
BRIDE	BLUE	GROOM
FEUD	PRICELESS	

WDF-4

Answers

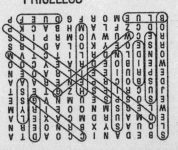

This summer, come cruising with Harlequin Books!

PORTS OF CALL

In July, August and September, excitement, danger and, of course, romance can be found in Lynn Leslie's exciting new miniseries PORTS OF CALL. Not only can you cruise the South Pacific, the Caribbean and the Nile, your journey will also take you to Harlequin Superromance®, Harlequin Intrigue® and Harlequin American Romance®.

- In July, cruise the South Pacific with SINGAPORE FLING, a Harlequin Superromance
- NIGHT OF THE NILE from Harlequin Intrigue will heat up your August
- September is the perfect month for CRUISIN' MR. DIAMOND from Harlequin American Romance

So, cruise through the summer with LYNN LESLIE and HARLEQUIN BOOKS!

CRUISE

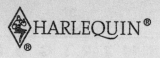

THE VENGEFUL GROOM
Sara Wood

Legend has it that those married in Eternity's chapel are destined for a lifetime of happiness. But happiness isn't what Giovanni wants from marriage—it's revenge!

Ten years ago, Tina's testimony sent Gio to prison—for a crime he didn't commit. *Now* he's back in Eternity and looking for a bride. *Now* Tina is about to learn just how ruthless and disturbingly sensual Gio's brand of vengeance can be.

THE VENGEFUL GROOM, available in October from Harlequin Presents, is the fifth book in Harlequin's new cross-line series, **WEDDINGS, INC.** Be sure to look for the sixth book, **EDGE OF ETERNITY,** by Jasmine Cresswell (Harlequin Intrigue #298), coming in November.

WED5

HARLEQUIN®

INTRIGUE®

A Decade of Danger & Desire

**Harlequin Intrigue invites you to celebrate
a decade of danger and desire....**

It's a year of celebration for Harlequin Intrigue, as we
commemorate ten years of bringing you the best in romantic
suspense. Stories in which you can expect the unexpected...
Stories with heart-stopping suspense and heart-stirring
romance... Stories that walk the fine line between danger
and desire...

Throughout the coming months, you can expect some special
surprises by some of your favorite Intrigue authors. Look for
the specially marked "Decade of Danger and Desire" books
for valuable proofs-of-purchase to redeem for a free gift!

**HARLEQUIN INTRIGUE
Not the same old story!**

DDD